Stu
Truly

STU TRULY

DAN RICHARDS

 YELLOW JACKET

 **YELLOW JACKET**

An imprint of Bonnier Publishing USA
251 Park Avenue South, New York, NY 10010
Copyright © 2018 by Dan Richards
Jacket illustration by Simini Blocker
All rights reserved, including the right of reproduction in whole or in part in any form.
Yellow Jacket is an imprint of Bonnier Publishing USA, and associated colophon is a trademark of Bonnier Publishing USA.
Manufactured in the United States of America BVG 0618
First Edition

10 9 8 7 6 5 4 3 2 1

Library of Congress Cataloging-in-Publication Data is available upon request.
ISBN 978-1-4998-0646-5
yellowjacketbooks.com
bonnierpublishingusa.com

To the NYBA Trailblazers Team:
thanks for reminding me what it's
like to be twelve

Let me start by saying I believe in telling the truth. It's just that sometimes the truth is complicated.

For instance, if you happen to staple your finger to your seventh-grade history assignment, you might be tempted to yell, "I'M BLEEDING OUT!" But that kind of truth might upset those in your class who faint at the sight of blood. Instead, it's better to say, "Please excuse me while I go get a tissue. And a bucket."

And if your vision begins to blur, it's best not to slump to the floor whimpering, "Mama, hold me. I'm heading for the light." Not because your classmates are squeamish about dying, but because your best friend, Ben, will repeat it to you every day for the rest of your life.

Sometimes the truth can seem obvious, until suddenly it's not. For example, I eat meat. I'm pretty sure if you checked kids' lunches everywhere you'd find meat in most of them. There would, of course, be the occasional peanut butter sandwich and perhaps a lunch or two filled with nothing but candy, but I'd bet you'd never find anything remotely resembling tofu, grilled vegetables, or Greek yogurt. I'm not saying there isn't a place for such things. I'm just saying I can't think of a place and doubt I ever will.

Being truthful about eating meat seemed like a no-brainer until the day Becca showed up. She and her family moved to town to be near her grandmother and get out of the "rat race," she explained her first day in class.

I can't really say I was paying attention. A new girl in school was about as interesting as, well, another girl in school. It wasn't until she finished that our eyes met for a moment. That happened to be the moment I was stapling my history assignment.

The next day at lunch I found everyone gathered around Becca. Before her lay the most unnatural lunch

I had ever seen. Something thin, limp, and red had been cruelly placed between two slices of bread so dark they looked like they'd been colored with a permanent marker. "What is that?" I demanded.

"A roasted pepper sandwich," one of the girls whispered.

"Roasted what?" I could feel the bile creeping up my throat.

"Pepper," Becca confirmed. "It's amazing on rye bread with brown mustard. Anyone want to try a bite?" She looked up at me with eyes as big and round as Oreos.

"Sure," someone said, someone who sounded a lot like me.

Becca tore off a piece and held it out. "Okay."

I stared down at the dark mass, wishing I could learn how to keep my own mouth shut.

"Mama, hold me. I'm heading for the light," Ben whispered from behind.

Taking a deep breath to keep from punching Ben, I shoved the bite in whole. This was a mistake. My tongue found itself wedged up against two cardboard-like pieces of bread. Jutting out from between them was something slimy that I could only hope was the roasted pepper. I wanted to gag.

"What do you think?" Becca asked.

I tried to swallow, but the bread refused to budge. Meanwhile, the pepper slowly slithered around my mouth like a snake searching for sunlight. "Mmbbfthl," I mumbled. I reached down and grabbed the nearest drink and took a swig. Just my luck, it was lemon-lime soda. The bubbles sizzled, agitating the bread into a swollen rage. The foam expanded into my throat. I tried to hold it down, but instead, the chain reaction exploded like an atomic bomb. The next thing I knew, kids were running in all directions screaming, "Ooh, gross!" and "That's disgusting."

I finished my coughing fit to find Becca sitting all alone at the table with a mixture of soda, bread, and flecks of pepper strewn around her like the wreckage of a tropical food storm.

I grabbed a couple napkins and tried to wipe the table. "I'm sorry," I sputtered.

"Are you okay?" she asked.

Considering I had just spewed food all over her sweater, her concern came as a real surprise. I wiped my mouth with my sleeve. "Uh, yeah," I lied.

"I take it you didn't like it."

I kept my distance from her eyes. They were unnerving. "No, it was great," I lied again. "It was really great."

"No, it wasn't."

I threw the napkins into the trash. Both fell short. I bent to retrieve them. "Yeah, it was good. Kinda nutty tasting. My family eats stuff like that all the time."

Becca dumped the remainder of her lunch into the garbage can. "Really? Is your family vegetarian?"

Warmth spread up the back of my neck. *The truth. Stick to the truth.* "Yes."

She beamed. "That's so cool. My family, too."

I ran to get a mop, racking my brain for the answer to the question *Why did I just tell her I was a vegetarian?*

When I got back, Becca was gone. I leaned

against the table. In the last few minutes, I had made an important discovery. Sometimes the truth is complicated. And sometimes it's downright impossible.

Something told me I was in trouble. Deep trouble.

My full name is Stuart Cornelius Truly. My father likes to joke that he wanted to name me Yours, as in Yours Truly, but I know he'd never do something like that. I don't think. My mother is the one who picked the name Stuart. As a child, she was a big fan of the novel *Stuart Little*. She couldn't get over the idea how cute it would be to have a mouse for a son. Unfortunately, my mother got a boy for a son. She named me Stuart anyway.

It didn't take long for kids to find out where my name came from. By the middle of first grade, I was known as Stuart the Little. By second grade, just the picture of a mouse was enough to send me into a rage. In third grade, my teacher shortened my name to Stu after a boy brought a copy of *Stuart Little* to class. I went after him with a math book and a dry eraser.

I have no memory of it, even after they showed me the dent in the dry eraser. From that day on, I was known only as Stu, or sometimes That Crazy Kid with the Dry Eraser. Mostly they just called me Stu.

For the remainder of the afternoon, I stayed as far away from Becca as possible. There was something about her that made my stomach knot up, and not like when you're going to throw up, either. That kind of knot has a purpose. This knot just sat there refusing to budge. Maybe I was allergic to her. I had heard of such things before. Ben once read a book about a boy who became allergic to his dog. Eventually, the boy discovered his dog was an alien trying to take over the world. It was a good book. I should have read it.

PE gave me the perfect chance to get some help thinking things through. Every Tuesday we did a fitness run around the school. A fitness run meant sprinting until we were out of Mr. Snedaker's sight, then slowing to a crawl so we could talk with our friends.

I joined my usual posse. "Do you think being a vegetarian is cool?" My eyes darted like a cornered rabbit. "No reason. Just curious," I threw in for good measure.

"Not if your friends are vegetables," Ben said, giving me an elbow.

"My dad's crazy. He thinks vegetarians are a cult," Tyler said.

"Cult? Seriously?" Ben replied. "They *eat* vegetables, not worship them."

"That's not what my dad says," Tyler explained. "He thinks vegetarians worship animals like chickens and stuff."

"No one worships chickens," Ben said. "Not even chickens."

"I hate chickens," Ryan said, spitting. "I pray every day our chickens will run off so I don't have to clean up after them anymore."

Ben's face lit up the way it does when he's just remembered a fact bound to make everyone else wish he hadn't. "I once read in *Ripley's Believe It or Not* about a guy who kept dozens of chickens in his house. He even slept with them and everything."

By this point, I had to accept I would get nothing useful from these guys. Should have seen that coming.

"Okay," I interjected, "how is it my dog will eat

9

something dead on the side of the road but avoid a cooked carrot I drop on the floor?"

Ben bumped my shoulder. "Smart dog."

"Amen," I agreed.

"Hold up," Ben said. "Time to look like we've been running."

Ben led us to the drinking fountain, where we took turns splashing water on each other to give the impression we were sweating. It was a nice touch—so long as Ben didn't get carried away. We sprinted the final corner and raced to where Mr. Snedaker was addressing the rest of the class. How they'd gotten back ahead of us was a real mystery.

"Don't forget we start our unit on nutrition next week," Mr. Snedaker said, eyeing the hand-shaped sweat stains Ben had plastered on my shirt. "You need to keep a journal of what you eat between now and then. Make sure you record each food and what food group it belongs to. Bring your journal in on Friday."

After the bell sounded, Ben and I walked together to our next class.

"What food group do Oreos go in?" Ben asked.

"I don't think they've discovered that food group yet," I said.

"Then what do I put for breakfast?"

"Well, if you eat them with milk, maybe you can call them cereal. I think there's a food group for cereal."

"Good idea. What do you have in the morning?"

"Cereal."

"That's too bad. Maybe you can come over for *cereal* at my house Saturday."

I grinned. "Sounds good."

"How's your finger doing?"

I looked down at the bandage. "It's okay. My butt still hurts, though, from the shot they gave me."

"They gave you a shot in the butt because you stapled your finger?"

"Yeah, with a really big needle. I guess a staple can infect your butt."

Ben looked entirely too excited about the idea. "An infected butt would be nasty. I'd like to see that."

"The doctor says I'll be fine in a few days."

Ben let his shoulders droop. "That's too bad. Just think if your butt turned all green and nasty."

We stepped through the doorway into our next class just as the bell rang. For once in my life, I was thankful Ben would need to be quiet.

At dinner that evening, my father read the sports section of the paper as usual. He liked to say you could get all the news of the day just by reading the sports section, if you knew how to read between the lines. Apparently my mother didn't. She peeked down at the front page lying next to his plate.

"This is interesting," she said.

"Mmm," my father replied.

"It says right here that the president and his wife will be celebrating National Vegetarian Day next week."

My ears perked up.

"What's a vege-table-man?" my five-year-old brother, Tommy, asked.

My mother gave him the sort of smile you give an infant after they've just dribbled milk bubbles down your shirt. "A vegetarian is someone who doesn't eat meat."

"Wait," I cut in. "Are you saying the president is a vegetarian?"

My mother gave me a knowing smile. "Yes, both the president and his wife are vegetarians."

My father and I choked at the same time. The sports section slipped to the floor. As did my cooked carrots. Chester, our dog, immediately turned away.

"What is wrong with people these days?" my father muttered. "It's unnatural."

It should be noted that besides being the world's foremost authority on barbecuing, my father also owns Truly Meats, the only butcher shop in town. That might explain why he was holding his half-eaten pork chop before him like a crucifix.

"Frank, there's nothing wrong with vegetarians. Doctors say we should all eat more vegetables and less meat."

My father crossed himself with the pork chop.

"I like meat," my little brother blurted in an act of solidarity.

"Dang right you do," my father encouraged. "Can

you believe someone came into the store the other day asking for vegetarian meat loaf? It's *MEAT* loaf for crying out loud."

My mother rolled her eyes. "Stu, will you help clear?"

I stacked my brother's plate on my own and dumped them into the sink. Why on earth had I told Becca my family was vegetarian? Nothing could be further from the truth. If my family were stranded on a desert island with nothing to eat but vegetables and sand, we'd be eating sand morning, noon, and night. There's lying and then there's *LYING*. I was pretty skilled in the art of lying, but *LYING*, that was a whole different matter. Lying required altering a few details in your life. *LYING* required relocating to another state and changing your name to Armando.

Maybe it wouldn't come up again. But I knew better. The things I want to avoid most in life always come up again.

"Stu," my mother called from the dining room. "Don't forget to clean up the carrots you dropped on the floor."

See? Always.

After cleaning up the pile of orange mush formerly known as my carrots, I retreated to my room. I got out my homework, but my mind kept wandering.

The simple choice was to avoid Becca at all costs. That seemed easy enough. I had been avoiding girls my whole life. It wasn't a conscious act, more of a habit I had never questioned before. Yes, they took up desks in class, but other than that, they were like homework—best avoided. Why then be concerned? Deep down a little voice told me this was different. But why? There seemed no logic to it.

My mother stopped in with a plate of cookies. Not just any cookies, either, Oreos. The cookie made in heaven by other cookies, and that's without even bringing milk into the equation. I fell asleep that night soothed by their crunchy sweetness. Sometimes a little sweetness does a body good.

4

I woke the next morning to discover the dark cloak of death had descended on me during the night. I could barely lift my head off the pillow to call for help. Or breakfast. My mother hurried upstairs with bacon, eggs, and a thermometer.

"Ninety-nine point one," she said, reading the thermometer. "You're not exactly dying."

"It feels like it," I croaked through a mouthful of egg.

She left the tray on the floor and went to call the school, mumbling something about how in her day only pneumonia kept a child home.

I managed to keep breakfast down, even the second helping. But the effort left me exhausted. I lay back and closed my eyes, trying to get some much-needed rest before lunch. Grilled cheese would take all my strength. In the stillness, my mind wandered.

I found myself in the opening scene of my favorite video game, *Death Intruders*. Everywhere I turned, putrid-smelling zombies with bad teeth and rotting limbs chased me. I ran into a dark forest, hoping the evergreen scent would cover my irresistible flesh smell. As I wandered about, a cabin appeared. Near the back was a small window. Peeking through it, I saw a dingy room with a single light bulb hanging from the ceiling. Hiding in one corner crouched Becca. Her frightened eyes told me all I needed to know. I tested the window. Locked. The back door was locked, too. Using my daydreaming strength, I lifted the entire door off its hinges. Daydreaming strength is the best.

Becca's eyes widened as I entered the room where she had been hiding. I motioned for silence. My keen hearing detected zombies coming down the hall. With catlike reflexes, I slammed the door on the first one. As he slid to the floor, I leapt into the hallway. The second swung a rotting arm. I ducked under it, then launched my foot into his groin. He fell with a whimper.

I took Becca by the hand, pulled her from the cabin,

and led our escape into the woods. When we were safely away, she pulled me to her, wrapping her arms around me.

"Thank you," she whispered.

At that moment, my mother arrived with lunch tray in hand. "Oh my, you're sweating. Maybe your fever is breaking." She placed her hand on my forehead.

Maybe I was sicker than I thought. Something was wrong with me. What other explanation could there be for daydreaming something like that? My mother sat on the edge of the bed and stroked my head. I needed to talk this thing out. I opened my mouth. "Is that wheat bread on my grilled cheese?"

My mother let out a sigh and headed back downstairs with the tray. "White bread coming up, Your Highness."

The next day, Ben was waiting for me when I got to school.

"Feeling better?"

"Yeah, I guess."

"Lucky. You got to stay home for a day."

"Yeah, lucky."

"At least you don't have to do your oral report in history today." Ben lowered his voice. "You won't believe what I have to tell you."

"Does your dad have that foot fungus again? My mom burned the last pair of socks I wore to your house."

"No," Ben said. "Better."

"Better than foot fungus?"

Ben giggled. He can giggle like a girl. And he

appreciates when I point that out.

"Shut up. My dad bought *Death Intruders 4.*"

"Really? That's awesome! Can I come over?"

"Duh, that's why I'm telling you."

Having something like *Death Intruders 4* to keep me distracted was the best way to avoid thinking about something else that kept making my palms sweaty. I almost didn't notice Becca the rest of the day, except when I glanced over to see if perhaps she'd turned into an alien while I was gone. Unfortunately, she hadn't.

After school, Ben and I half walked, half ran to his house. Fighting zombies has always relaxed me. Even when they were trying to eat my brain for the umpteenth time. If only zombies walked the real earth, I'd be a lot calmer. Any worries that had dogged me the day before were quickly forgotten amid the simple pleasure of roaming about with a chain saw in a post-apocalyptic zombie world. By the way, post-apocalyptic is a fancy word for a place like Disneyland but with better rides and shorter lines.

Unfortunately, the moment I left Ben's house that evening, my troubles returned. I had not gone more than half a block when I ran into Becca. Ben had neglected to tell me Becca lived on his street. A best friend should know better than to keep something like that secret.

Becca waved. "Hi, Stu!"

The last image from my daydream sprang to mind. My heart thundered like it was a zombie warlord preparing to burst from my chest.

"Hi, Becca," I squeaked.

Becca fluttered her eyes just as she had after our escape into the woods. "Are you okay?"

My face grew hot. Was I okay? How was I supposed to know? The zombie warlord didn't think so. He was beating on my rib cage like an undead jackhammer. I forced my eyes to the ground. "Yeah, fine. Great. Good. Never b-better," I stammered.

Becca giggled. "That's good. I think."

She turned and fell in step with me as I tried to keep both feet moving. "Do you like it here?" Becca asked.

The question caught me off guard. "Yeah, I guess so," I replied. "I've never lived anywhere else."

Becca kicked a rock. "That must be nice. We've

moved every two years my whole life."

I imagined moving to new places all the time. The zombie warlord let out a groan and took a seat. "Must be hard making new friends all the time."

"Yeah." Becca kicked the rock again. It just missed my kneecap.

"Probably would be easier if you didn't try to kill them." I kicked the rock back. It bounced off her shoe. "Oops, sorry."

"And I thought I was the killer around here," she quipped coolly.

I let out a snort, and not the kind of snort you make when you're trying to blow a penny back out one nostril. This was the surprised kind of snort you make when you've just discovered girls can be funny.

I grinned. "I've killed a few in my day. The town used to be a lot bigger."

Becca stopped as we reached the corner. "See you tomorrow," she said.

I risked meeting her glance. "See you tomorrow."

She turned and headed back in the direction we'd come, her ponytail bouncing behind her.

I replayed our conversation over and over in my mind as I walked home. There wasn't really a lot to replay, but the more I did, the more each moment held a life of its own. The way her wrist shook when she waved hello. The slightly upturned curve of her lips when she spoke. How her eyes grew larger as she listened. I had been best friends with Ben my whole life, yet I couldn't recall one feature of his face. Why? I didn't have an answer.

The next day at lunch, I made the mistake of sitting at the same table with Ben. Not that this was unusual. The unusual part was that Ben was sitting at a table full of girls. As I walked up, he and Kirsten, a girl from his English class, were having a deep discussion about reptiles.

"There's a guy in *Ripley's Believe It or Not*," Ben was explaining, "who had his tongue surgically altered so it looks like a snake's."

"Ooh," said Kirsten.

"And he had his body tattooed to look like scales."

Kirsten leaned in. "My grandmother's boyfriend has a lizard that rides around on his shoulder, even when they go to the movies."

Ben dropped his half-eaten sandwich. "No way.

That's so cool. I want a Gila monster I can walk on a leash."

I sat down next to Ben. Across the table, I noticed a cup of yogurt, a salad, and a bag of something that looked like dried peas covered in red pepper. I looked up to find Becca munching on a handful of the peas.

"Hey, Stu," she said, holding out a pea in her hand. "Ever had Joe's Smokin' Peas? They're really good."

I took the pea and held it between my finger and thumb. "Looks good," I lied. I put the pea in my mouth. It felt as hard as a piece of gravel. Flakes of red pepper latched onto my tongue like biting fire ants. I gulped it down against my will. It left a trail of fire all the way to my stomach. "Mmm, tasty," I choked out.

"I love them," Becca replied. "Better than candy."

Comparing peas to candy was like comparing school to vacation. The two shouldn't even be used in the same sentence. I jammed a hand into my lunch bag and discovered a leftover pork chop, apple slices, and a hard-boiled egg. The apple slices were for show, but the rest of it was pretty much a perfect meal. And then I looked at the yogurt, salad, and peas of fiery death across from me. I was now a vegetarian. Or so Becca thought. I let go of the pork chop and pulled out the apple slices. "Want one?"

"Oh, those look good." Becca took a slice and bit off a dainty piece.

Ben would've shoved the whole thing in his mouth, bag and all. Instead, I heard him still discussing reptiles with Kirsten. "I like Gila monsters because they're the only venomous lizard native to the United States."

"Really?" Kirsten replied, her attention locked on Ben. I had never seen anyone's attention locked on Ben before, not even mine—and I was his best friend. Something seemed out of place.

"Yeah," he continued, "they live in the southwest and can eat just about anything, even horses and stuff." Strangely, Ben's head appeared to be swelling larger. I rubbed my eyes. It had to be the cafeteria lighting. His head couldn't get any bigger. He was like one of the dwarves from *The Hobbit*. He once tipped over while watching a beetle crawl between his feet.

"What else did you bring?"

I looked up to find Becca staring at my lunch

bag. "What else did I bring?" I peeked inside at the remaining contents. "Uh, well, I have a—a—" Was a hard-boiled egg vegetarian? I couldn't remember. "Actually my mom gave me money to buy lunch," I said, staring down at the brown paper bag clutched in my hands.

Becca's eyebrows wrinkled. "Oh . . . I didn't know they had any vegetarian entrée options."

I looked up at the cafeteria reader board. *Today's menu: Hamburger or chicken strips with french fries.*

The zombie warlord in my chest woke up and began pounding to get out. I very much wanted to free him so he could find someone else's chest to pound on and leave me to die in peace. Neither of us got what we wanted.

I rolled the top of my lunch bag down tightly and got up. "Excuse me, I'm going to go buy some milk." I then turned and made a beeline for the exit. Once outside, I ran to the boys' room and locked myself in a stall.

In case you've ever wondered, this is not a good place to eat lunch. Unless there is a girl in the cafeteria who thinks you are vegetarian—in which case, a stall in the boys' room is a perfect place to eat lunch. By holding my nose with one hand and feeding myself with the other, I was able to get most of my pork chop down. The hard-boiled egg was a lost cause. It went in the trash along with the apple slices.

For the remainder of lunch, I hunkered down in the stall and tried to ignore the thought of what boys normally do in the bathroom, none of which made keeping lunch down any easier. By the time the bell rang for class, I was a deep shade of green. With what little dignity remained, I staggered from the boys' room and slumped my way to history class.

I should've stayed in the bathroom.

7

History is my least-favorite subject. Not because I dislike learning about dead people. (Since I began playing *Death Intruders*, I've become quite obsessed with the dead.) But because I'm stuck sitting next to Jackson. Not only is he tall for his age, he's the only guy I know with an actual chin hair. The way he strokes it, you'd think there was a gerbil attached to his face. To make matters worse, he goes around in muscle shirts. Just because he actually has muscles doesn't mean he needs to show them off like some sort of circus freak show. If I had muscles, I would keep them neatly tucked inside my T-shirt where they belong. I wouldn't stand there posing while giving my oral presentation on the Incas.

Normally, Jackson's behavior wouldn't bother me

except for one small fact. Becca's desk sat in the front row. After the lunchroom incident, I was once again doing my best to ignore her, but that plan wasn't working. If anything, the more I tried, the more my attention went right back to her. The only saving grace was that my desk sat in the back of the classroom, where Ben couldn't see my gaping stares. Were that to happen, I'd be introducing myself as Armando at my new school somewhere east of the Rockies.

Jackson finished his oral report to a smattering of applause, none of which came from me. The only smattering I cared about was the smattering of hair on my arms so downy soft that my forearms could be mistaken for a newborn chick. Man, I hate puberty and the way it changes people. Other people. I looked up to find Jackson taking his seat.

"Pretty good, huh?" Jackson whispered.

I hunkered down in my chair. "Uh, yeah. I guess."

"When are you going?" he asked.

When was I going? What was he talking about?

"Stu, you're up," Ms. Hunzinger called from the head of the class.

Up? Up what? And that's when it hit me. With the events of the last few days, I had forgotten all about my oral report.

"I don't think there's enough time," I tried.

"There's still forty-five minutes of class left. Now let's get on with it."

My thoughts swirled. I hadn't done the reading. Or listened well enough to Jackson to know what he'd read. I had no excuse, at least none I was willing to give in front of the class. The door caught my eye. I could probably make it out before my teacher could stop me. But where would I go? Just call me Armando.

"We don't have all day, Mr. Truly."

I rose from my desk and walked to the front of the room like a man being dragged to the gallows. If only my head were being chopped off, it would be so much easier. But my life is never that quick and painless.

"The Incas lived a long time ago," I began. I paused, reaching deep inside for something I knew about the Incas. I came up empty-handed. "They lived in groups and invented a lot of cool things." Beads of sweat formed on my forehead.

"Can you give some examples?" Ms. Hunzinger prompted.

"Yes, of course," I replied without enthusiasm. "They made clothing and cooking utensils." I was pretty sure all ancient people had done that. "And invented ink." This was a stretch, but with a name like the Incas, it only followed.

Giggles rose from the class. "And they built ships." This had to be true. What ancient civilization didn't build ships? Laughter fluttered about. Apparently, at least one civilization hadn't.

"Mr. Truly, have you done any research at all on the Incas?"

My sweatshirt smelled like something had crawled inside and died. From the corner of my eye, I could see Becca with her eyes down.

"Not any I can remember at the moment."

"Shall we try again Monday?" Ms. Hunzinger continued. "I think I know how you'll be spending your weekend, am I right?"

I slunk back to my seat.

"Bummer," Jackson said, the muscles of his jaw

33

rippling. Even his jaws could ripple. He handed me a couple books. "Read these, they're really good."

I looked down at *The World of the Incas* and *Incas: Then and Now*. Muscles, facial hair, and smart. He was a downright menace.

I arrived home red in the face, having packed thirty pounds of books about the Incas with me.

"Hey, Stu," my father said, surveying the multitude of shiny objects lying around him, none of which seemed likely to be connected together any time soon. "I'm starting on the carburetor today. And then it's on to the handlebars. Wanna give me a hand?"

When my father's stressed, he disappears into the garage to rebuild his motorcycle. He says he's customizing it, but I don't think he has any idea how to put it back together.

"Sorry, I've got homework."

He squinted at me. "Something bothering you?"

Was something bothering me? Excellent question. I wanted to tell him I had eaten my lunch in a bathroom stall, but that would only lead to more questions, none of which I was ready to answer. "Nope."

He squinted harder, scrunching up his face like a pirate in some old movie. "Is it a girl?"

"No," I said, my eyes going wide and my face turning red like a stoplight.

"Don't let them get to you," he said with a wink. "They've got their wily ways, but so do we."

I left my father and lugged the books I was carrying up to my room. After an hour, I had yet to open one of the books but had spent a lot of time reflecting on what sort of wily ways boys had in dealing with girls. So far I hadn't thought of any. I figured spending more time on the matter wouldn't change things. After another hour, I concluded I was right. By then, it was almost dinnertime. My stomach grumbled a reminder that I had only eaten half my lunch.

For dinner, my mother had made baked chicken with potatoes and gravy. My father liked to call potatoes the meat of all vegetables. This seemed to make them more appetizing. I had to agree. Trying to eat broccoli was like trying to down a small tree, but a potato in any form was downright tasty.

"Your father said you have a lot of homework this weekend."

"Yeah," I replied between mouthfuls, "we're studying the Incas right now. I have to give an oral report on Monday."

"Oh," my mother said, "that sounds important. If you'd like to practice it, just let us know."

My father let out a sigh, the sort of sigh I'd let out if I were being forced to listen to a speech on the Incas. Just today in class, I had let out several such sighs.

"Bill," my mother said sternly, "I'm sure your father listened to you practice your oral reports when *you* were in school."

My father gave my mother a have-you-met-my-father? look. "Not unless the report was on the location of a hidden fishing hole."

"Well, still," my mother continued, "if Stu needs to practice, we can take a few moments to listen."

"Really," I interjected, "I'm okay."

"Good man," my father said with a wink. "Have another potato."

After dinner, I skimmed through chapter after chapter of interesting facts about the Incas. When I say *interesting*, I mean interesting to others. Apparently, my teacher qualified as one of those. Jackson seemed to be another. That in and of itself ruined the subject for me. I took a moment to check out my bicep. As always, it made my shirt bulge, so long as I pulled down on the sleeve from underneath with my other hand. Unfortunately, I had to pull down hard to get any bulge at all. Over time, all the pulling had stretched the sleeve of my T-shirt to the point that it looked like a woman's blouse. I checked the bicep of my other arm. The phrase *nothing to see* popped to mind. That is not the phrase you want when flexing your bicep. I went back to my notes.

Actually, I didn't go back to my notes. I spent the rest of the weekend doing pretty much what I always did on the weekends, despite my mother's gentle reminders that Monday would be here "all too soon." All too soon seemed all too far away while playing *Death Intruders* at Ben's, eating junk food at Ben's, and playing more *Death Intruders* at yep, you guessed it, Ben's house.

Sunday night I concluded that my mom was right. Monday really was coming all too soon. And at the rate I was going on my report, summer school would be coming all too sooner, which landed me back in my bedroom staring at the notes I never really started Friday evening.

I returned to flipping through the books on the Incas I had been ignoring. And that's when a miracle took place. I discovered the Incas were the first to farm potatoes. Now that was something. The Incas were also into brain surgery. I myself had an interest in brain surgery, having removed a few brains from zombies while playing *Death Intruders*. I scribbled notes frantically, suddenly fascinated by Incan civilization. For several long minutes, actual learning took place. I think I heard angels sing.

After finishing my report, I wandered downstairs looking for a snack. In the refrigerator, I found the lunch my mother had packed for me. I took a peek to ensure all the proper food groups had been covered. What I saw was a masterful mixture of protein, grains, fruit, and candy. She had outdone herself by including both a chocolate chip cookie and a Halloween-sized bag of Skittles.

I was about to close the fridge when the memory of my lunch Friday struck me. Should I end up seated near Becca again, I would be left with half an orange as my main course. The clear answer was to sit on the far side of the lunchroom, where a guy could eat his baloney sandwich in peace. But following that plan of action would require my body doing what my brain commanded. Of late, that had been a real problem. I'm not sure my body had been following anything going on in my head. In fact, the more my brain tried to lead, the less my body seemed to follow. I was beginning to wonder how I accomplished anything at all.

I removed the sandwich from the bag and slid the baloney into the garbage. Mayonnaise left a trail of what looked like slug slime down the side of the garbage bag as the baloney slipped from view. Having no idea what one puts in a vegetarian sandwich, I slipped the first vegetables I found between the slices of bread and put it back in the bag. A wave of relief swept over me. I would be able to eat my lunch tomorrow seated at a table with everyone else and not alone on a toilet.

My mother tucked me in that night, though I had been asking her not to for over a year, and left me with a good-night kiss on the forehead. I fell asleep dreaming of zombies, a cabin in the woods, and another heroic rescue.

At lunch Monday I found myself once again near Becca. Not because I meant to sit near her, but because Ben seemed completely unaware of who or where he was. Only days before, he had been a well-adjusted kid who knew lunch was to be had with his buddies. In the span of a few days he had turned into some sort of lunchroom psycho interested only in discussing lizards and other trivial gossip with Kirsten. Being the true friend that I was, I felt obligated to support him despite his mental state. That is how I found myself sitting across from Becca. Being a best friend is filled with sacrifices.

Spread before her was a colorful mixture of vegetarian delights. There were green peas, cheese wedges, fresh fruit salad, and a bar of chocolate large enough to keep her afloat in the event of a flash flood.

"I've been thinking about the cafeteria food," Becca said as I sat down. "They really should have a vegetarian entrée option every day."

"You're right," I agreed.

I pulled out my sandwich and laid it on the table with pride. Today, we were equals. Today, we were two people with a shared passion for vegetables. Today we—my inner dialogue stopped short as I followed Becca's eyes. My sandwich appeared to be with child. Several children. I lifted the bread to take a better look. Whatever possessed me last evening had been of the devil. Between the two slices of bread I found three brussel sprouts, a whole carrot, and several uncooked lima beans.

"What is that?" Becca asked.

"Um—I'm not exactly sure," I said, closing the slice of bread before anything crawled away. "My mom likes things real natural," I sputtered.

"Is she into raw foods?" Becca asked, pulling her lunch closer, as if fearing the contents of my sandwich might be planning an attack.

"Uh yeah, I guess so." I had no idea what she was

talking about, but if it explained what was hiding between my two slices of bread, I was more than willing to run with it.

"My mom is into raw foods, too. I like being vegetarian, but I can't go that far."

"Yeah," I agreed. "But what can I do? She's so proud of me for trying."

Becca smiled. "That's sweet. You must really like your mom."

I was starting to blush. The important thing about lying is to own it no matter how much your stomach is turning. "Yeah," I said.

"That's so sweet," Ben added. "Not only does he love his mother, he also enjoys cooking and tending to his flower garden. Oh, and he just adores those quizzes in the back of *Seventeen* magazine."

I gave Ben a playful punch in the arm, the kind of playful punch that knocked him off his seat. He got up, giggling.

"Ben's real funny," I explained. "And he giggles like a girl."

"My brother giggles like a girl," Kirsten added, "and he's in high school."

"I don't giggle like a girl," Ben said with a giggle.

"Yes, you do," we all agreed.

This set off both of the girls—and Ben—giggling uncontrollably. As the only one who does not giggle, I confined myself to a brief snort followed by a guffaw.

"He's giggling," Kirsten said, pointing at me.

I could only hope the rest of the lunchroom had gone deaf or died.

When the bell sounded, the four of us trooped out of the lunchroom together. We reached class far too soon, still giggling for no reason known to mankind.

Becca and I parted at the door. "See you later," she said.

I floated to the back of the room like a balloon half full of helium.

"Mr. Truly, would you care to give your oral report?" Ms. Hunzinger asked as she brought the class to order.

I immediately rose. "Yes. Yes, I would." I boldly strode to the front of the room and positioned myself almost but not quite in front of Becca. "The Incas were an amazing people known for many things," I began. "They were excellent farmers who loved growing vegetables. They terraced the hillsides and grew tomatoes, avocados, peppers, strawberries, peanuts, squash, sweet potatoes, beans, pineapple, and bananas." From the corner of my eye, I could see Becca smiling.

When I finished, I returned to my seat with a self-satisfied smile. In my life, there have been three moments in which time seemed to stand still. Two of them had occurred in the last ten minutes.

10

The word *vegetarian* began cropping up everywhere I turned. The nightly news did a story about the health benefits of a vegetarian lifestyle. My mom brought home a bag of corn chips that proclaimed *Vegetarian Approved*. And my father continued to receive requests at work for vegetarian meat loaf, veggie burger patties, and even meatless weiners. It was almost more than he could take.

"All this vegetarian talk," he blurted out one night at dinner. "How is a guy to make a living these days? Our country is going to the dogs."

My mother looked up from her green beans. "Is business down?"

My father avoided eye contact. "Maybe a bit," he mumbled. "Can you believe there are people who think meat is bad for you?" He shoved a piece of sirloin the size of a footstool into his mouth.

My mother lifted her juice glass. "There are still lots of people who eat meat."

My father coughed. Something that might have passed for a calf being born spewed onto his plate. "They need to be reminded that meat is American. People were eating meat long before anyone ever heard of a vegetable."

"Yeah," my brother added. He took a big bite of his steak and spit it out.

"Tom Neville Truly," my mother snapped. "You will *not* spit your food onto the table, no matter what example your father sets."

"Listen to your mother," my father said. "And don't waste a perfectly good piece of steak."

My brother crossed his arms. "It was fat."

"That's what makes you big and strong," my father replied.

"And fat," I threw in. At least one of us had taken a health class.

"People need to be reminded. There has to be a way

to get their attention back on what really matters," my father said.

"You mean meat?" I asked.

"Yes, meat. We're made to eat meat," he continued. "You know, to hunt game and roast it over an open fire—"

"When was the last time you hunted anything?" my mother interrupted.

"It's not about hunting," my father continued, staring off into space. "It's about being who we were meant to be."

My mother rolled her eyes, then cleared her plate and left him sitting at the table, still staring into space, the trace of a smile curving his lips.

I left the table, too, and went straight to work on my health journal. By *straight to work*, I mean after a short detour to play *Death Intruders 3*, followed by a few moments of Internet browsing on my mother's computer and ending with a slow trudge up the stairs, while inspecting the banisters for defects in workmanship. About 9:00 p.m. I sat down at my desk and got out my notebook.

I started with the protein food group, as this was the easiest for me to remember. In the last few days, I'd eaten bacon, chicken, steak, lunch meat, pork chops, and nearly a hard-boiled egg. Next, I reviewed my dairy intake. Milk and cheese jumped to mind, lots of milk and cheese. Then came grains. I wrote down breakfast cereal and bread. After that, I was left with fruits and vegetables. Things were getting trickier at this point. I was pretty sure I'd eaten at least two apple wedges and maybe a slice of orange or two along the way. I rounded off and wrote down apple and orange.

That left me with just vegetables. Hmm . . . what vegetables had actually passed through my lips? I had looked at plenty enough vegetables in the last few days and placed several between two slices of bread. And been involved in more vegetable discussions than I cared to remember. But I could only list the ones I'd actually eaten. I wrote red pepper and peas. Oh, and potato. Thank God for potatoes. And thank God for the Incas for discovering how to farm them. This was almost a religious moment for me.

I looked back over my work. Clearly, I was eating

a well-balanced diet with plenty of the things that mattered most and tasted best. Why fruits and vegetables had to be included was beyond me, but to each their own.

I packed up my notebook, congratulating myself on a job well done. After brushing my teeth, I climbed into bed and prepared for another night of zombie adventure and damsel-in-distress rescue. And not just any damsel. Becca.

11

The next day in PE, Mr. Snedaker filed us into the gym. We took seats in the nearest bleachers. "Please take out your food journals," he said.

I was happy to see that some of my classmates seemed unprepared. I, on the other hand, slipped my journal from my backpack. The cardboard cover felt warm in my hands. The notebook was of a good weight, sturdy and filled with promise. Well, at least the first page.

"Hopefully, you've been keeping careful track of what you've eaten the last few days. Were you surprised?"

Not in the least. When you've got a diet as complete as mine, you know it. I wasn't about to take any chances and throw in ill-advised surprises. "Stick to the basics" is a motto I live by. I had just made the motto up, but it seemed pretty mature for a guy wearing sneakers and basketball shorts.

"Well, let's find out," Mr. Snedaker continued. "Becca, would you tell us what you put for protein?"

Warmth spread up the back of my neck. When had she joined our class? That girl was everywhere. And right at the moment, that was not a good thing.

"Okay," she replied. "I was a little confused about the categories. Do nuts go under vegetable or protein?"

"Excellent question," Mr. Snedaker responded. "Nuts go under protein."

"Okay. In that case, I put peanuts, tofu, cheese, and yogurt under protein."

"Very good," said Mr. Snedaker. "No meat?"

"My family is vegetarian."

"Very good. We could all stand to eat less meat." Mr. Snedaker turned in my direction with an all-too-pleasant smile on his face. "Stu, what about you? What did you put down under protein?"

I glanced down at my journal. The warmth slowly spreading up my neck turned into a wildfire ready to burst out of my ears. My list of proteins looked exactly like what it was: all meat, all the time. "Uh, I also had a question," I said, trying to buy time. "Are all nuts considered nuts or are some vegetables?"

Ben tipped over. He did an admirable job of not giggling out loud, though the rhythmic pounding of his fist on the bleacher was a bit distracting.

"Yes, all nuts are considered nuts," Mr. Snedaker said slowly, as if speaking to a toddler.

I stared back down at my journal. The same entries were still there. No matter how many times I blinked, the words refused to change. "Well, in that case, I had peanut butter on my nuts." Something didn't sound quite right about how that came out.

The class erupted into a chorus of laughter led by Ben, who was rolling about like the demon child from a movie we watched one time during a sleepover. I swore off going near all demon children after that night. Watching Ben reminded me why.

"Okay," Mr. Snedaker said, holding up both hands in an effort to get the class's attention. "Mr. Truly, that is not the behavior I expect in this class. I'll be seeing you after school in detention."

Detention seemed a reasonable price to pay to keep the truth hidden from Becca. As class continued, I discovered I was not the only one who was uncomfortable discussing the contents of their journal. Ben, for instance, was called on to read his list of grains. The word *Oreos* slipped out before he could catch himself. Tyler included M&M'S in his list of dairy products. And Ryan listed gum as a vegetable.

By the time everyone had taken a turn reading from their journals, Mr. Snedaker looked a bit ashen. "I can see," he said, "you have a lot of room for improvement in your diets. I want you to continue keeping your food journal for the remainder of the semester. We'll read again from them near the end of the term. Let's see if your food choices change for the better between now and then."

Well, at least there would be no more reading from our journals for the time being. I let out a sigh of relief. Maybe things weren't so bad after all.

Mr. Snedaker continued. "Well, Monday is what you've all been waiting for." He paused for effect.

We stared innocently.

"We begin the square dancing unit," Mr. Snedaker finished, just as the bell rang.

No one spoke as we filed out of the gym. My hands were sweating for no apparent reason.

Once outside, Ryan turned to us. "Why do we have to do square dancing? Why can't we just play dodgeball or something fun?"

"It's all part of their plan," Ben said matter-of-factly.

"What plan?" I asked.

"My mom says the school does things like this to socialize us into being respectable young men and women," he explained.

Tyler shook his head. "What's respectable about square dancing?"

Ben shrugged. "I don't know."

"Do you think we'd get detention if we refused to participate?" I asked.

Ben bumped my shoulder. "You can't even read out of your journal without getting detention."

He had a point.

12

After spending a pleasant hour in detention, I got home to find an old flatbed trailer in the driveway. My father walked around it like a king surveying the location of his future castle. Chester joined in by peeing on both wheels as if getting a head start on the moat. From my viewpoint, all I saw was trouble in the making.

My mother confirmed my suspicion. "What in the name of heaven are you doing with that old trailer?" she asked, having just pulled into the driveway with a carload of groceries. What my mother lacked in tact, she more than made up for with righteous fervor. She approached my father like a priest exorcising Satan himself. "We are NOT buying a boat, another motor-cycle, or anything else that could possibly be put on that—that *thing*," she said, holding her ground despite the trickle of dog urine working its way toward her open-toed shoe.

My father raised both hands in a placating gesture. "Molly, trust me. Just be patient and all will be revealed in due time." His voice was so reassuring I was ready to believe him, though my mother seemed less inclined.

"If I see motorcycle parts or any other junk coming home on that trailer, you're going to be sleeping beneath this *thing* with nothing but the clothes on your back and a sign on your forehead that reads *Blockhead lives here.*"

"Molly. I would never do something like that. Trust me, this is something special, you'll see."

My mother let out a grunt that could've passed for a grizzly bear's. She hefted the groceries out of the car, all six bags' worth, and waddled her way into the house, still grunting.

My father looked at me. "She's a heck of a woman, Stu. Let me tell you—one heck of a woman."

I was dying to know what he intended to do with the trailer but I could see he was lost in thought. He had returned to pacing, a smile on his lips identical to the one I'd seen the night before. I left him there in the driveway, a man and his trailer. Something big was brewing. Or not. Only time would tell.

Saturday morning began with a leisurely breakfast of pancakes and bacon.

"Stu, you must have a wife and children living in there," my dad said, pointing to my chest, "the way you're eating these days."

"Don't give him a hard time," my mother scolded. "A growing boy needs the calories."

My father shook his head as I took another piece of bacon. "He needs to get on with it while there's still enough livestock in the world to feed him."

"I want livestock, too," my brother added, thinking only of himself as usual.

"Don't worry," I said with a pat on his arm. "I may get all the bacon, but there will always be plenty of broccoli for you."

My brother grabbed at the remaining bacon on the plate. The plate flipped off the table and clattered to the floor, sending the last piece of bacon skittering beneath my brother's chair. Chester moved with the reflexes of a tiger. The bacon disappeared before anyone could form the word *no*, let alone *bad dog*.

"I want more bacon!" my brother yelled.

"See what happens when you torment your little brother," my mother said, handing him the remaining piece of bacon on her plate. "The two of you are enough to drive me crazy."

"What about the trailer in the driveway?" I asked innocently.

My mother stopped with a bite of pancake halfway to her mouth. "Fine, the three of you. And let's not even go there," she said. She pointed her fork in my father's direction. "That topic is still under review."

My brother chomped his bacon down in one bite like the dog. He smiled at me, bacon grease glistening his lips. "Grr," he growled.

I ate my last four pancakes and excused myself.

Up in my room, I reviewed the load of homework

that had been heaped on me before the weekend. My math, English, science, and history teachers had apparently masterminded a diabolical plan to ruin my days off. If I started now, I could be done by June. Using time travel, I could then return to the past and turn in all my assignments on Monday. Whether to work first on my homework or a method of time travel perplexed me. I opted to head over to Ben's house.

As I neared his street, I found myself slowing. This seemed strange since usually I sped up the closer I got to his house. Ben and I had known each other since we were babies. Even when I couldn't stand the sight of the guy, I'd always rushed to get from my house to his. Except today. Today, I ground to a halt a full two blocks from my destination. And there I stood, hands at my side and a bewildered expression on my face. What was I doing? For a moment, a pang of fear shot through me. I wasn't feeling guilty about ditching my homework, was I? The thought made my hands go cold and a chill run up my spine. It couldn't be that. What, then?

An image flashed to mind. I tried to shut it out,

but it returned. An image of a girl. *The* girl. Becca. I was beginning to sweat. The zombie warlord in my chest woke up. I suddenly realized I was standing in the middle of the street in front of Becca's house. Panic exploded within as I retreated behind a parked car. My eyes glanced toward her porch, perched up off the street like the prow of a mighty ship. Empty. The steps leading up to the porch, empty. The front windows, empty. Nothing to worry about.

"What are you doing hiding behind that car?" Ben asked from behind me.

I nearly jumped out of my skin. Why would a best friend do something like that? I tried to clear my brain and push her from my mind. To lie to my best friend, I needed all my wits about me. "I don't know," I croaked at last.

"You're freaking me out," he replied. "Are you spying on Becca or something?"

The zombie warlord hammered out a warning in Morse code on my ribs. I took a breath. It would feel good to admit the truth. "No, of course not," I said with all the earnestness I could muster. "You've got to be joking. I don't even like her." This was probably going a bit far, but I was over the edge by this point.

"Oh," Ben said, his voice sounding anxious. "Yeah, I don't like anyone, either."

I paused. I hadn't suggested he did. Why would I? He was Ben. He didn't like girls. I nearly spit out my tongue. He didn't like girls, did he? I wasn't ready for the implications.

"Wanna play *Death Intruders 4*?"

The look on Ben's face changed from anxiety to relief. "Yeah, of course. I made it to level fourteen," he said eagerly. "There are zombies everywhere. Wait till you see."

I risked a last glance back at Becca's house. Maybe it was only a reflection, but I thought I saw movement within. I returned my attention to Ben. "Cool."

The next few hours passed quickly. Somewhere along the way, between levels, we ate chips, devoured candy, and drank a half liter of orange soda. By midafternoon, my vision had blurred and my thumbs were beginning to cramp. Also, Ben's mother had discovered the pile of books on his desk. She leapt to the conclusion that he needed to take a break from "playing silly games" and do something "that really matters." I've never understood how a mother in her right mind is unable to see the relevance of a game where you learn how to defeat a zombie apocalypse. Do they think zombie apocalypses defeat themselves? Just because we've never had one doesn't mean there isn't one just waiting to happen. As carefully explained in *Death Intruders 1*, a zombie apocalypse is only a bad batch of wieners away. Ben and I have been boycotting hot dogs ever since. But as long as others keep eating them the best we can do is prepare ourselves for the worst. And hope it happens in our lifetime.

The walk home was uneventful, despite pausing at the corner for about twenty minutes. To be clear, I was not waiting for anyone to happen by. I was simply a young man hanging out on the corner being cool, while glancing around to make sure Ben didn't see me.

When I finally got home, I found my father and his friends circled around the trailer. When I say friends, I mean the guys my father plays cards with once a month and whom my mother refers to as his "hick buddies."

My favorite, Harley, waved hello as I approached. He was not only named Harley but he rode one as well. He had already promised I could take it for a spin as soon as I was strong enough to hold it up. Considering the bike's weight, I would need to become a circus strongman first. However, that didn't prevent my mother from forbidding it. "I'll be dead and gone before I'm gonna let you go riding a Harley," she liked to say.

"Hey, Stu," Harley said, "what you been up to?"

I stopped next to him. Harley was about six foot five and probably weighed 280. He had a handlebar mustache and low-slung sideburns that perfectly complemented his greasy black hair. He brushed back the strands hanging over his eyes.

"Not much," I replied. "Just been over at Ben's playing *Death Intruders 4*. We made it to level eighteen."

"Dang," he said. "I can't get past level four."

My father walked up and put a hand on my shoulder. "Stu, we were just talking about you."

"How come?"

He leaned in. "We've got an idea for the trailer that might need your help."

"Really? Does Mom know?"

My father's hand slid back like a vampire exposed to sunlight. "Your mother's not here," he said quietly. "For now, let's keep this to ourselves, shall we?"

"No problem," I replied, "as long as you give me some idea what's going on."

My father stepped back and inspected me like a crime boss looking over a new recruit. At last, he gave the others a knowing smile. "Okay," he said. "This is just between you and us, but we're going to build a float for this year's parade."

Of all the possibilities that had run through my mind since the trailer appeared, a parade float had never been on the list. A parade float? Seriously? I checked everyone's faces. They were all grinning from ear to ear.

I nodded weakly. "A parade float. Excellent."

My father puffed out his chest. "Yep. Just you wait and see."

I looked again at the trailer sitting in the middle of the driveway. "How are you going to keep this a secret from Mom?"

My father gave a knowing look to his cronies. "Oh, don't you worry about that. We've got it all worked out."

I shook my head and walked into the house. Sure they did.

14

Our town is known for its annual Irrigation Festival. You may have heard of it. Probably not. Long ago, irrigation ditches were dug to bring water into our valley from a nearby river so crops could be grown.

Apparently that was a big deal back then and the reason Sequim, pronounced like "squid" but with an *m* at the end, grew from being an unknown town in western Washington to being a slightly less unknown town. These days, there's not much in the way of farming going on. Mostly people move here to retire. As my father likes to say, Sequim is a great place to die. My second-grade teacher told me that was a "disturbing" viewpoint after I used it to explain why my grandmother had recently moved to town.

The high point of the festival is the Irrigation

Parade. The parade takes place on the first Saturday in May. People come from all over. They line Main Street hours in advance, sometimes parking overnight in campers just to reserve the best views. The parade is filled with all the sights and sounds our small town has to offer, including marching bands, clowns, drill teams, dog clubs, clowns, 4-H exhibits, more clowns, and, most important, floats.

People in Sequim love their floats. They'll spend months converting an old hay truck into a thing of beauty with flowers, streamers, sparklers, and sometimes even moving parts. One year, there was a float that looked like a flower garden with a giant papier-mâché bumblebee chasing a papier-mâché butterfly. Unfortunately, that year a storm hit. By the time the float reached us, the bee looked more like a pile of runny dog poop and the butterfly had melted down into a pair of flyswatters sticking out of an old boot.

Personally, I've never found parade floats the least bit interesting. They seem to be more about celebrating the town's royalty and carrying church groups singing "That Old-Time Religion" than about entertaining those of us under the age of sixty. Were I to see a float with live explosives on it or zombies rising from the dead, I might feel differently. But that never happens. For the most part, I just ignore them and focus on the good parts of the parade such as the cotton candy, the occasional clown tripping, and, well, mostly, the cotton candy.

At dinner, I did my best to respect my father's wishes concerning secrecy. It wasn't easy. Especially after he used the mashed potatoes, bratwurst, and string beans on his plate to build what looked like a miniature parade float.

"What are you doing?" my mother asked.

My father gave me a quick wink. "Oh, nothing. Just playing with my food."

My brother stuck three beans in his mashed potatoes and began clubbing them with his bratwurst.

"I think it's time the shop needs some new marketing," my father said.

My mother directed my father's attention to the slow death being inflicted on my brother's green beans. "Do you see what he's doing?"

"Don't club your beans," my father said.

"I'm playing with my food," my brother replied, still clubbing his beans.

"Don't play with your food," my father said.

My brother crossed his arms. "It's not fair."

My father took a large bite out of what had been the bed of the trailer. "See? Just eat." He speared another bratwurst from the serving platter. "I'm thinking of doing something that will really grab people's attention."

My mother's eyes widened. "Does this have anything to do with that trailer?"

My father jammed the bratwurst slice into his mouth along with the last of the mashed potato wheels. "Now where would you get *that* idea?"

My mother shook her head. "Just promise me that trailer will not be used for anything other than hauling things."

"You have my word," he replied, almost too quickly.

My mother looked him up and down. "You better be telling the truth."

"Scout's honor," he replied with a reassuring smile.

"You were never a scout."

"Hmm," my father murmured. "Ain't that the truth."

The remainder of the weekend was consumed with homework and time spent mulling over the mystery of the secret parade float. Not that I really spent much time on either. To be honest, I don't know where the time went. Anyway, Monday came way too soon and PE class way too soonest of all. I found myself pressed against the gym wall with the other boys.

"I can see you're all excited about our unit on square dancing," Mr. Snedaker said.

Mr. Snedaker clearly misunderstood the meaning of *excited* since it was the last word any of us would choose to describe square dancing.

"I promise none of you will die from the experience."

Who was he kidding?

"And you might even enjoy it, if you give it half a chance."

The odds of us giving it *half a chance* were about as good as the odds we would suddenly sprout a beard and leg hair. I, for one, would die for some real leg hair, the kind that can be seen without magnification. But that wasn't happening anytime soon. Currently, my downy soft arm hair was perfectly matched by my downy soft leg hair.

"So, go ahead right now and grab a partner."

Say what? Me and all the boys pressed up against the wall trying to deny the reality of what was happening, while the girls took to gathering in small groups for protection. They peered about periodically while whispering among themselves. A few made eye contact, daring one of us to leave the safety of the wall. Instead, we clung to it like metal shavings to a magnet.

Just when it appeared Mr. Snedaker would be forced to back down from his misguided attempt to socialize us, a lone figure stepped away from the wall and crossed into no-man's-land. He had the broad shoulders and the lone chin hair of one already moving on a different plane from the rest of us. He approached the nearest clump of wide-eyed, not-quite-invisible girls. Then, in a single sentence, he altered the course of our middle school history.

"Wanna be my partner?" Jackson asked.

"Yes," Becca answered.

The zombie warlord in my chest lurched sideways, pounded one final, disgruntled *thump* on my ribs, then clambered out my backside and slid under the nearest set of bleachers. My other organs twisted together in a failed attempt to follow. When your organs turn against you, you know you're in trouble.

In the meantime, a flurry of activity took place around me. Boys asked girls, girls asked boys, Ben asked Kirsten. Ben did *what*? Had I just witnessed my best friend asking a girl to be his dance partner? My life flashed before my eyes. That wretched mostly man, Jackson! How could he do this to me? I had half a mind to yank that lone chin hair out and shove it up his—

"Do you want to be my partner?"

76

I spun to find Gretchen Gorst standing beside me. I remembered Gretchen vaguely from the last seven years of going to school together. Honestly, I'd never given her much thought. Just like all the other girls I had gone to school with for the last seven years. All I knew was that I'd rather be slowly eaten by a tag team of crocodiles than forced to hold hands with Gretchen while prancing around inside the gym. "Uhhhh, sure," I stuttered.

She let out a sigh of relief. I think she said something but my attention had returned to Jackson standing next to Becca. The neon gym lights made her skin look slightly green, but it was the most amazing green I had ever seen. Unlike Jackson, whose skin looked like the infected wieners that had started the zombie apocalypse in *Death Intruders 1*. I wished I had one of those wieners so I could sneak it into his lunch. We'd see who got the last laugh then.

"Okay, now that everyone is paired up," Mr. Snedaker said, raising both hands to get our attention, "it's time you got acquainted with your partner."

I didn't like the sound of that at all. Since when did

we have to talk to them? This was getting serious.

"I want you to take a few minutes and get to know each other. Find out your partner's interests. What do you share in common?"

What did we share in common? Who cares? I was sure she didn't spend her afternoons playing *Death Intruders*. Beyond that, I really didn't want to know.

"Do you like to dance?"

I turned to find her staring at me with expectant eyes. "Um—not really."

"Oh. I love to dance. I've been taking lessons since first grade."

I noticed the gym windows had not been cleaned in a very long time. If someone gave me a bucket and a sponge, I was more than willing to hang like a spider from the ceiling and make those babies shine. I'd even be okay to hang from the ceiling and lick them clean with my tongue. Anything to stop this conversation.

"What do you like to do?"

What I'd like to do is run screaming from the gym and then be run over by a car in the parking lot to end this nightmare. "Um, I like to play video games."

"Oh," she said. "Do you like music?"

Did I like music? Was that really a question? "Sure."

"Oh," she said for like the five hundredth time. "I like Christie Moreno. She's cool."

I had no idea who Christie Moreno was. Nor did I want to find out. Unless Christie knew how to get me out of here or was willing to run me over in the parking lot. "Yeah, she's cool."

"Well, class," Mr. Snedaker interrupted. "How's it going? Discovering things in common?" He slithered through the jungle of nervous couples like a boa constrictor looking for prey to suffocate. He stopped next to Jackson and Becca. "How about you two? What have you found in common?"

Becca smiled. "We both have younger sisters who drive us crazy."

A ripple of nervous laughter passed through the class.

Mr. Snedaker turned next to Ben and Kirsten. "Excellent. What about you two?"

Ben giggled. "We both like lizards."

"Interesting," Mr. Snedaker commented. "And how

79

about you two?" he said, staring directly at Gretchen and me.

"We both like Christie Moreno," Gretchen said with enthusiasm.

The girls giggled, as did many of the boys, apparently those familiar with her music. Some went so far as to double over with laughter. "She's a teen idol," I heard kids whispering. "Little girls love her." This led to more laughter. I was pretty sure they weren't laughing at Gretchen. If only a car would smash through the wall of the gym and crush me against the bleachers. Sometimes a guy can't buy a break.

When class finally ended, I staggered out the doorway gasping for air. What had happened in there? My palms were sweating so badly I thought they were melting.

Tyler bent next to me, his cheeks flushed. "Thank God that's over."

Ryan staggered past looking as if he'd seen a ghost.

"Ryan!" I called out.

He tried to open his mouth, but no words came out. Poor guy.

"I'm done with PE," Tyler lamented. "It's not worth it."

I tried to give him a pat on the back, but my hand didn't have the strength. "Yeah, I'm stuck with Gretchen."

"Gretchen? You're lucky," Tyler said. "I got Hannah. She doesn't smell right."

I had to admit for all Gretchen's faults, at least she bathed. That was something to hold on to. "Sorry."

"You think you got it bad?" Ryan said, having recovered enough to join us. "I'm stuck with Debbie. She must be at least a foot taller than I am."

That was mostly true. Debbie had to be at least six feet tall. Ryan barely topped five feet.

"That's awkward," I replied.

"At least she doesn't smell like an old folks' home," Tyler said. "I'm gonna need nose plugs."

"Yeah, at least your head won't be in her armpit," Ryan countered. "She's gonna rub me under her arms like deodorant."

"Hey, guys," Ben said, joining us with a grin so wide you'd have thought he'd just been pulled out of school early.

"Shut up," we all said.

"You're just happy 'cause you like the girl you got stuck with," Tyler said in his most sarcastic voice.

"Yeah, you're already boyfriend and girlfriend, aren't you?" Ryan added.

"Shut up," Ben shot back. "I don't like her. I just didn't want to get stuck with some freaky girl."

I parted from the group and headed for my sixth-period science class. Did he really not like Kirsten? I wanted to believe him, but I had my doubts. Anyway, what did it matter who he was partnered with? What really mattered was who I was *not* partnered with. I thought of how I'd just stood there against the wall like everyone else. Everyone except Jackson. He had walked right up to her while I just stood there gawking. I hung my head and turned a corner. Becca appeared from the opposite direction. We stopped short, but our notebooks kept going, tumbling in a pile.

"Oh, I'm so sorry," Becca said, reaching for the pencil that had landed between my feet.

"My fault," I said, leaning around her to pick up my notebook.

We straightened up at the same time, our eyes locking for a moment.

"See you," she said, brushing past me.

"Yeah," I replied, turning to watch her go. "See you."

I was still standing in the same spot when the bell rang, my brain reviewing statistics like a sports broadcaster. She wasn't six feet tall. She didn't outweigh me by fifty pounds. She didn't smell funny. And she didn't make me want to jump in front of a speeding car. Why hadn't I asked her to be my partner?

16

The next day at lunch, I made a point of sitting with Tyler and Ryan. Not because I was dying to have lunch with them, I just couldn't be at the same table with Becca. Or next to Ben talking lizard trivia with Kirsten. The fact that Jackson was sitting with them didn't help, either.

Tyler and Ryan were busy discussing our first day of square dancing.

"I'm not standing next to her for a whole hour," Tyler blurted. "She smells like my grandma."

"At least you're not her personal deodorant," Ryan replied, rubbing the top of his head.

"Everyone thinks I like Christie Moreno," I added with an appropriate sigh.

Tyler laughed. "I already thought that. You're part of the Moreno Tornado."

"What's that?" I asked.

"That's her fan club," Tyler explained. "My little sister joined. You get free stickers and stuff. I bet you have some on your binder."

I bit into my ham sandwich. At least I didn't have to pretend to eat anything vegetarian today.

"I'd listen to Christie Moreno any day if it meant not sticking my head in Debbie's armpit," Ryan said.

"Hey, at least it's not Hannah's armpit," Tyler said with a grimace. "You'd be dead before you hit the floor."

Ryan looked across at me then lowered his eyes. "Gretchen's not so bad."

I choked on a piece of ham. Something didn't quite sound right about that last comment. Maybe I was just paranoid, but I was starting to think my friends were becoming interested in girls. I shook my head to clear the thought. Ben I could understand. He'd always been a little against the grain. But Ryan? Ryan still picked his nose when he thought no one was looking. Ryan still drank milk with a straw. And still snorted like a donkey every time he laughed. Ryan couldn't possibly be interested in girls. Especially a girl like Gretchen. Gretchen, who liked Christie Moreno. Gretchen, who had the audacity to ask me to be her dance partner. Gretchen, who this very moment was staring at me from two tables away.

I choked down the remainder of my ham sandwich while secretly checking out the rest of the cafeteria. How many of the guys in this very room were secretly staring over at some girl hoping no one would notice? And how many girls were doing the same thing? Was anyone else staring at me? I felt exposed. At this very moment, there might be eyes boring a hole in the back of my head wondering if I wanted to join them listening to Christie Moreno.

My hands were trembling. It was too much to absorb. I needed air. My eyes were drawn to Becca. She sat quietly with her yogurt and her hot, spicy peas, seemingly oblivious to everything happening around her. She glanced up, our eyes met. I grabbed my lunch and bolted from the cafeteria without looking back.

17

The gym seemed smaller than usual as I stepped out from the boys' locker room. After leaving the cafeteria, I'd spent the remainder of lunch trying to shut things from my mind. So far, it'd been useless. It was like a secret world had been unveiled, one in which we were under some sort of alien control. Everything I had taken for granted I now questioned. Every glance, every laugh, every moment held secrets. I wished for a key that could decipher what was happening around me. Instead, nothing made sense.

"Hi, Stu," Gretchen said, smiling.

"Hi," I replied without enthusiasm.

"I hope this unit doesn't last long," she whispered. "I love ballet. It's real art. My teacher says that square dancing is just for people who don't want to take the time to learn how to really dance."

Hey, that sounded like me. "Yeah," I replied.

"Today," Mr. Snedaker began, "we're going to practice forming squares and getting lined up correctly."

Apparently, the square in square dancing is there
for a reason. Mr. Snedaker explained that four couples
together form a "square." This meant separating
into groups throughout the gym. Creating a square
with eight people who were trying desperately not
to make eye contact wasn't easy. Every few minutes,
Mr. Snedaker would repeat, "Gentlemen, she's not
going to bite." Clearly, he hadn't been with us on the
playground in first grade.

Just as we thought the worst was over, he had us
form new groups. This was enough to send some of
the boys over the edge. I ended up across from Ryan.
He looked like a little boy next to his mother. Debbie
was so large she could have pounded Ryan into the
ground like a tent pole. At the sight of Gretchen, Ryan
straightened up, almost enough for his head to reach
Debbie's shoulder. By the time we were all in our
correct positions, the bell sounded.

"Be prepared tomorrow," Mr. Snedaker called as we shuffled out, "for the real dancing to begin."

"That wasn't too bad," Ben said as we headed across the lawn to class.

"Are you out of your mind?" Tyler spat out. "I may never breathe right again."

"Shut up," Ryan said. "I look like a circus midget next to Debbie."

"That's true," I added.

"Maybe we should get together and practice after school," Ben said, laughing.

"Yeah, you can be the girl," Tyler said.

"That won't work," I added. "His head's too big."

Ben gave me a shove. "Mama, hold me. I'm heading for the light."

Sometimes the best thing you can do for your best friend is strangle him. If only his neck weren't so thick.

Ben giggled. "Thanks for the neck massage."

Really. How did I put up with that guy?

18

I got home that afternoon to find the trailer gone and my father waiting in the garage.

"Hey, Stu," he said.

"What happened to the trailer?"

My father flashed a mischievous grin. "It's at a top secret location disclosed only on a need-to-know basis."

"Do you mean like Harley's barn?"

The mischievous smile faded to a frown. "Remind me never to take you to anyone's house." He sized me up, then took out a measuring tape from his pocket. "As long as you're here, I need a few measurements." He approached and held one of my arms out to the side while he slid the tape from my wrist to my shoulder.

"What are you doing?" I asked.

He stepped back and wrote in a notebook. When

he finished, he squatted and measured my inseam. "Nothing much." The mischievous grin had returned. "Just measuring."

I could think of nothing good that could come from my father taking my measurements. "Seriously, you're not taking up sewing again, are you?" My father had the impulse one year to hand sew our Halloween costumes. I ended up in a costume that looked like Winnie the Pooh after a knife fight. My brother had it even worse. My father sewed him a tomato costume that came out looking like a diseased liver.

My father paused. "You'll see."

I headed inside. "Whatever it is, I'm not wearing it!" I yelled over my shoulder.

After a small snack that included two cookies, a bag of potato chips, and a quart of milk, I headed up to do my homework. Since that wasn't going to happen before dinner, I headed back down and got on my mom's computer. She had taken a part-time job at the hospital thrift store, so that meant I could browse until dinner without fear of being told I was wasting time. Clearly, I was wasting time, but the last thing I needed was my mother telling me that. I typed "Christie Moreno" into the search engine. A list of Christie Moreno sites, including the Moreno Tornado fan site, popped up. Against my better judgment, I clicked on the link.

I shouldn't have. For starters, a poster-sized image of Christie filled the screen. A girl barely older than me stood on stage in a fishnet-stocking jumpsuit that looked like she'd been wrapped in the neighbor's chain-link fence. Her eyes were black and blue with makeup. Beneath the blackened eyes were lips so puffed out she appeared to be having an allergic reaction to the feather boa wrapped around her neck. Beneath the image were the words *Christie rockin' it at the MTV Awards.* Further down were comments posted by her many Moreno Tornado fans. The same phrases repeated over and over, such as *You're the best, Love you,* and *I'll always be your #1 Tornado.* I was beginning to wish I'd had a smaller snack. My stomach churned from all the syrupy sweetness.

To the side were links to some of her hit songs. I clicked on one called "Make Me Feel You." The moment it started I recognized the tweener-bop beat. The song had been used on a commercial for Cheezy Pops cereal. No wonder the sight of it made me want to skip breakfast. Putting cheese flavor on cereal was bad enough. Add teen diva music and you had a lethal mix. I closed out the website. My head hurt. How could girls like something like that? I'd rather be eaten by piranhas in my own bathtub than forced to join a teen idol website.

I headed back upstairs and resumed my daily staredown with my textbooks. So far, the textbooks were winning. I idly opened one of them. Before me lay a folded piece of paper. *Stu* was written on the front. I opened the note. A girl's handwriting greeted me with the following: *I'm glad we're partners. We have so much in common. Looking forward to getting to know you better. Gretchen.*

I read the note again. Nothing changed in the second go-round. I half expected Ben to pop out from behind my door. I wouldn't put it past him to write something like that just to scare the living daylights out of me. But Ben was nowhere to be seen, and the note could not possibly be his handwriting. Ben's handwriting looked like a horse with a pen tied to one hoof. This writing had loopy flourishes like something my first-grade teacher would have done. I read the note for the third time. None of the words changed. She didn't like me, did she? The truth hit me like a zombie's fist to the forehead. I dropped the letter, hoping it would have the good sense to scuttle out of sight so I could forget it ever existed. The note just lay there, mocking me with its presence.

For the first time, I wished my parents had given me a cell phone. Not because I wanted the responsibility of keeping track of one. We all knew I'd lose it first chance I got. But I could have used a friend to talk to right now. And I didn't dare use the phone downstairs for fear of being overheard. I could walk to Ben's house, but that would take too long. Plus, I didn't want to be late for dinner. Hamburger night was not to be missed.

"Stu?" I heard from the hallway.

I turned to find my little brother standing in the doorway.

"Will you play with me?" A red towel hung off his

shoulder like a cape. In his hand, he held a sword made from the cardboard center of a paper towel roll. "I'm a knight," he said.

"Funny," I replied, slowly rising from my chair. I took one slow step forward then roared, "BECAUSE I'M A DRAGON!"

Sometimes life throws you a curve. And sometimes life sends you down the stairs impersonating a dragon thirsty for the blood of a young knight. Life is funny that way.

19

I got to school the next day to find Gretchen waiting outside. I told myself she was not standing there waiting for me, though the pit of my stomach said otherwise.

"Hi," Gretchen said as I passed.

"Hi," I replied, doing my best to avoid eye contact. I failed. Her eyes latched onto mine like a spy searching for government secrets. I strained to keep my mind shut, but her eyes wormed inside anyway.

Suddenly, she broke off the search and picked up her backpack. "I need to get to class," she mumbled.

I watched her go, feeling both guilt and relief. Part of me wanted to stop her. To say something to make her feel better. But I didn't. Instead, I took the long route to class so we hopefully wouldn't run into each other a second time again before the bell rang.

At lunch, I ended up at the same table with Ben. Not by choice. My legs carried me there entirely against my will. The smart thing would have been to sit with the guys and stay with my plan from yesterday. Why I couldn't just stick with that plan was a mystery. I sat down bemoaning my tuna fish sandwich that was about to go to waste. All I had left in my lunch sack was a handful of snap peas and a day-old butterhorn I had brought on the off chance I ended up near Becca.

"Hey, Stu," Becca said as I sat down.

"Hey," I replied, doing my best to maintain my cool. I wasn't really sure what my cool was anymore. It didn't help having Ben seated next to me.

He took one of my snap peas and flopped it around on the table like a dying fish. "Is your mother out to kill you?"

"She just wants me to be healthy."

Ben giggled. "Is that why she sent you with peas and a butterhorn?" Ben could be a real pain when he wanted.

"The refrigerator was short on leftovers." That was

true. Short on vegetarian leftovers.

"Exactly," Becca agreed, spinning my lie in a new direction. "That's why it's so important."

"Why what is so important?" I asked, taking the bait.

"That there be a vegetarian entrée option on the school lunch menu," she finished.

I looked up at the cafeteria menu board. It read the same as always: *Today's menu: Hamburger or chicken strips with french fries*. How I'd love a cheeseburger right now. "Yeah, you're right," I agreed.

"I knew you'd be with me on this," Becca continued.

Ben leaned over. "Becca wants us to do a sit-in to force the school to replace cheeseburgers with veggie burgers."

"Not replace," Becca corrected, "just add as an alternative."

Ben nudged my shoulder. "Wouldn't you prefer a veggie burger to a cheeseburger? You and your dad eat them all the time, don't you?"

I gently stomped on Ben's foot under the table.

"Yes, we love 'em," I lied.

"Oh good. Then you'll help us?" Becca asked with her biggest doe eyes.

"Of course," I replied.

"Ah, that's so sweet," Ben added. "I told her you'd be all into it."

His foot moved just before mine came crashing down on it with the force of a sledgehammer. That boy is quicker than you'd think.

"Hey," Kirsten interrupted, "there's a school dance this Friday night. Are you guys going?"

"Will they be playing Christie Moreno?" Ben asked. "If so, you can count Stu in. He loves to dance."

"So does Gretchen," Kirsten said, giving me a knowing look.

I lowered my half-eaten butterhorn. What was going on here? Why did she bring up Gretchen's name? I felt my ears beginning to burn. At times like this, I wished I could pull them off and stick them in a pocket. Maintaining my cool would be a lot easier with detachable ears.

"I've never been to a school dance," Becca said.

"Me neither," I replied. "They had a couple last year,

but somehow I forgot to remind myself to go."

Becca laughed. "Isn't it enough that we have to square-dance in PE?"

"Yes!" I exclaimed in agreement. "What's with all this dancing? Can't they just give us more homework? What's our school system coming to?"

That set everyone to giggling.

"I'm going to protest by bringing a textbook to read," Ben said.

That brought on more giggles. Apparently, the girls knew Ben better than I thought.

"We should all wear black," Kirsten suggested.

"And wear Mickey Mouse ears," Ben added. "We can be dancing Mickey Mouse ninjas."

The bell rang and we gathered up the remains of lunch.

"Don't forget," Kirsten said, "wear black Friday night."

I hadn't agreed to go, had I? I felt torn between the part of me that was excited Becca wanted me to go and the part of me that was terrified I might actually have to dance with her. I stood up to find

Gretchen staring my way. She quickly turned without making eye contact.

Gretchen continued to ignore me during PE, which became increasingly uncomfortable since we were standing next to each other. Each time we formed a new square, her posture grew more rigid. To make matters worse, Mr. Snedaker had us practicing our first movement. This involved taking hands in a circle and rotating counterclockwise before re-forming our square. For me, this meant an hour of holding hands with a girl whose icy touch sent shivers up my spine.

"Are we having fun yet?" Mr. Snedaker asked near the end of class.

Seriously? The looks being given should've wiped the grin off his face. I, for one, was contorting my forehead in such a way the word *scowl* could be read from space.

"Tomorrow we'll work on our swing technique," Mr. Snedaker called as he finally dismissed us.

"How am I supposed to swing Debbie?" Ryan lamented as we headed to our next class.

Ben caught up to us. "Square dancing is pretty cool, huh?"

The three of us eyed a passing garbage can. It seemed to be just Ben's size.

"Are you crazy?" Ryan snapped, scrunching his body to look almost big enough to be scary.

"I don't know what your problem is," Ben replied. "It beats doing health."

"I don't know," Tyler said. "I think I'd rather learn about the male reproductive system."

That brought shudders.

"Okay, maybe not," he continued, "but there has to be something better we could be doing. They don't make people in the real world go around holding hands with each other."

"Lighten up," Ben said, suppressing a giggle. By *suppress*, I mean not in any way suppressing his giggle. "You're taking this whole thing a bit too seriously."

"Too seriously?" I shot back. "Are you kidding? She wrote me a note." I stopped short. How on earth had I let that slip out?

A collective gasp occurred. In fact, I'm pretty sure the entire school gasped given how loudly I had proclaimed that last sentence.

"She wrote you a note?" Ben said, suppressing another giggle. "What did it say?"

"Nothing. It said nothing." I desperately wished for removable ears. At the moment, they were glowing so hot Santa could use them to guide his sleigh.

"Dude," Tyler interjected. "She's got a crush on you."

"Are you sure the note was from her?" Ryan asked quietly.

I glanced at Ryan, the memory from lunch a couple days ago returning. Oh no, not more drama.

"I don't know, probably not. It was just a note."

"Stu's got an admirer," Ben called out to some passing eighth graders.

"Will you shut up?"

"You the man."

"Shut up!"

Jackson happened past as we neared the classroom doorway.

Ben motioned my way. "He's the man."

Oh yes, compared to Jackson I was *the man*. Yeah, right.

20

Friday ranked right up there between getting my first filling and the time I crashed my skateboard into a rosebush. For starters, square dancing went from bad to worse. Gretchen refused to hold my hand while we maneuvered through increasingly complicated movements that required the artistic skill of someone actually trying to dance. With her hand shriveled up her sleeve like the head of a frightened turtle, I was forced to cling to the back of her sweater. This did not go unnoticed. I was referred to as Preschool Stu by my buddies for the remainder of class. It didn't help matters that Ben kept whispering, "He's the man," to anyone within earshot every time we passed.

On the way to our next class, I stated the obvious: "Square dancing sucks."

"Oh, don't be so cranky," Ben teased. "You the man."

"Shut up."

"I don't want to be Debbie's armpit hairbrush anymore," Ryan added.

Ben perked up. "She has armpit hair?"

"More than you."

"That's not saying much," I commented.

"Shut up, I have hair."

"Yeah, on your butt," I clarified.

"Anyone going to the dance tonight?" Ben asked to change the subject.

Tyler and Ryan stopped short.

"Are you kidding?" Tyler said. "After square dancing all week? I'm not going anywhere near a dance floor."

"Me neither," Ryan said.

I kept my mouth shut. I still wasn't sure what I was going to do. The idea of voluntarily going to a dance went against my better judgment. And yet I didn't want to let Ben down. From what he'd told me earlier, he had even gotten a black T-shirt to wear. Really? The only black thing I owned was a pair of basketball shorts with a bright orange stripe down the side that made me look like one of the school traffic cones. Beyond that, the closest I had to black was a dark blue T-shirt with the words *Don't Be a Butt* blazoned across the front that Ben had given me for Christmas. Ben thought it was funny. My parents, not so much. I had been forbidden to wear it in public.

I got home to find my father in the garage with a needle, thread, and piles of skin-colored material piled around him. "Hey, Stu, you're just in time."

From the looks of it, I was anything *but* just in time. "What are you doing?"

My father picked up one of the piles. "I need you to try this on."

He handed me something that looked like a jumpsuit made of women's nylons. "You gotta be kidding. I'm not putting this on."

My father set down his needle and thread. "C'mon, I just need to know if it's the right size."

I stared again at the skin-tight garment. "No way. This looks ridiculous."

"C'mon," my father coaxed. "It's not finished. When it's done, you're gonna love it."

I lowered my backpack and unfolded the garment.

It didn't look any more inviting than it had when bunched together in a wad. "Why don't *you* wear it?" I responded.

My father laughed as he held up another pile. "I will be. Trust me, we'll be the highlight of the parade."

Say what? "These are for the float?"

"Of course," my father answered, as if any fool could see that. "What did you think I was making? Pajamas?"

Frankly, the thought had crossed my mind. "No, it just doesn't look like a costume."

My father shook his head as if I were the most simpleminded person in the room. I was pretty sure I wasn't. "It doesn't look like a costume yet because I'm not finished. Just you wait and see. We're all going to look awesome!"

"What do you mean *all*?"

"You know, you, me, Harley, and the boys. All of us. We're going to be a hit!"

Riding on a float with Harley and the boys? I had to admit it sounded kind of intriguing as long as I didn't think about it too much. I didn't. I pulled the leotard on over my clothes.

"Perfect. You look perfect."

I pulled the thing off and headed inside. The phone rang as I entered the house. I had no doubt who was on the other end of the line.

"Hey, I just want to make sure you're going to the dance tonight," Ben said.

"Yeah, about that—"

"Dude, you have to come. I'm counting on you."

I paused, trying to think of an excuse that would satisfy Ben. Not that he'd accept it, whatever it was. "My dad needs my help with a project he's working on," I began.

"No, he doesn't. Your dad never needs your help with anything. Just put on something black and come tonight."

A different tact was needed. I didn't have one. "Okay, okay. I'll try to make it."

"You better be there. Or I'll hunt you down."

It's important to note, when Ben says he'll hunt you down, he means it. He once hunted Tyler down just to give him a return noogie on the head. Tyler was in church at the time. Ben escaped before the ushers caught him. He's surprisingly agile for a kid with such a big head.

"Okay, I'll be there."

This left me two hours in which to search for something black to wear. The search ended with me wearing the traffic cone-striped shorts and Ben's dark blue T-shirt hidden beneath my coat so my parents wouldn't notice.

21

My mother pulled her car up to the curb next to the gym. "I'm proud of you," she said before I could get the door open.

"Uh, okay," I responded.

She reached across and pushed a few strands of hair into place. "A first dance is a big deal."

I shrugged my shoulders. "It's just a dance," I squeaked out.

"Really," she said, looking me over. "Just a dance? Is that why your right leg is so jittery?"

I forced my leg to stop bouncing up and down like a pogo stick. "I don't know."

"Don't worry," she said. "Just give it a chance and everything will be all right."

Easy for her to say. When was the last time she went to a middle school dance? "Okay."

She gave me her best reassuring smile and motioned to the door. "Well, you better go in. You don't want to miss out."

I seriously did want to miss out. I could be home watching pointless reality TV right now. But it was too late to chicken out. I opened the door. "See you."

My mother gave a parting wave and drove off, leaving me alone on the sidewalk wondering why Ben and I hadn't carpooled together. A low rumble emanated from the gym. My stomach knotted. I took a last gulp of fresh air and made my way inside.

Considering what the last week had been like, I fully expected Gretchen to appear at my side. To my relief, she was nowhere in sight. Neither was Ben. I clung to the wall and tried to get my bearings. The lights had been turned off. In their place, a large disco ball hung from the center rafter. Flecks of light danced around the room. In the far corner, a guy wearing headphones and a tux jacket stood behind a pile of equipment. His head bounced to the beat while his fingers tapped on the laptop in front of him.

The current song ended and another began. The

new song sounded pretty much the same as the old song, a pounding beat that threatened to dislodge my liver and bounce it out through my gaping mouth. I had never heard music played so loud.

"Hey, Stu," someone yelled in my ear.

I turned to find Ryan beside me. "What are you doing here?" I yelled back.

"My parents made me come," he yelled in return. "What?"

I turned the volume on my voice up to ten. "I didn't say anything," I screamed.

"You didn't pay anything?" Ryan yelled.

"Say anything," I repeated, shouting as if he were standing a mile away.

"What do you want me to say?" he shouted.

I returned to scanning the room. Kirsten and Becca entered and immediately headed in our direction. They were wearing matching black tops and jeans. Next to them, I looked like the odd kid in class that wears checkered shirts with paisley pants.

Kirsten leaned in so close her lips actually touched my ear. "Where's Ben?" she yelled.

I shrugged.

"Oh well," she yelled again. "Let's dance."

Ryan and I were pulled onto the dance floor. There was plenty of room to spread out but we stayed shoulder to shoulder in order to hear each other.

"This is fun," Kirsten shouted.

I nodded. Apparently most of those in attendance were missing out on the "fun." They were clustered against the wall like newly hatched flies. I wished I could join them.

The girls hopped up and down like a pair of rhythmic gymnasts. I tried to mimic them but ended up looking more like a frightened rabbit. Ryan, on the other hand, gyrated about as if having a music-induced seizure. I had never seen anything like it from him before. What he lacked in skill, he more than made up for in righteous fervor. If only Ben had been there, we could have teased him about it for the rest of his life. I did my best to lock the memory away for the both of us.

After what seemed like a lifetime, the girls finally grew tired of all the hopping about.

"Anyone want something to drink?" I asked.

"That would be great," Becca shouted.

I grabbed Ryan and pulled him with me through the side door into the cool night air. My ears were ringing so loudly it sounded like bees were nesting inside. "Where's Ben?" How could I kill him if he didn't have the decency to show up?

Ryan gulped down a cup of lemonade. "I don't know. Who cares?"

Who cares? I cared. He had dragged me into this. And now he wasn't even taking the punishment with me. Why hadn't I thought of that? Pretend like you're going, then don't show up. Brilliant.

We headed back inside. Just as we were grabbing lemonade for the girls, a new song started. A different sort of song. With a slow beat. And a husky voice that crooned something about holding the one you love. My palms began to sweat. I froze in place. An idea formed. I should ask Becca to dance. What? No way. Maybe . . . I just needed to ask.

Just then, a lone couple walked out onto the dance floor. The lone couple took hands and rocked slowly back and forth. The lone couple seemed lost in a world only they shared. The lone couple was Jackson and Becca.

The cup in my hand hit the floor. Lemonade splashed everywhere. I barely noticed. All I saw was Becca holding hands with Jackson in front of the whole school—well, at least a small segment of the school. I wanted to run from the gym, but my feet were stuck to the floor. Maybe it was the lemonade. I stood watching Becca turn slowly in a circle with Jackson until she was staring right at me.

Suddenly, my feet found traction and bolted, taking me with them. Unfortunately, they bolted in the wrong direction. I ended up in a corner of the gym where the exit doors were locked. Why I couldn't turn into the Hulk at a time like that was beyond me. If only I could have, I would have smashed through the wall and run home with no memory of anything that had happened.

I turned and slowly made my way back to where I started. Kirsten came up to me with her hands on her cheeks.

"Are you okay?" she asked. "I thought you were going to run right through the wall."

The last thing I felt at that moment was okay. "Yeah, just needed some fresh air. A door would have helped."

She laughed, then grew serious, her eyes narrowing. "Next time, if you want to dance, just ask her."

Her words sounded ridiculous. And all too accurate. I had been stupidly slow. Again. But what was I to do? I'd never asked a girl to dance before. I didn't even know there was going to be a slow dance. Let alone what one was supposed to do during one. Once, Ben and I watched a movie where there was a high school dance. Boys and girls were hugging each other. What if I had tried to hug her? What if in front of the whole school I had done something completely embarrassing? I wasn't ready for this. I wasn't ready for any of it. I wasn't ready for hair or muscles or dancing or anything else that happens when your world is changing faster then you can keep up with.

The song ended, and the DJ picked up his microphone. "Hey, everyone! Thanks for coming out tonight! Hope you had a great time! Until next time, peace out."

The lights came up. A sea of kids shuffled for the

exit, pulling me with them. I gulped in cold night air as I exited from the gym. I had survived my first middle school dance. Barely. It was like something had been left behind in the gym. Some part of me. Oh, and my coat. Ugh. I swam back against the tide into the gym and found my coat wadded up in a pile of other forgotten coats. One of them I recognized. Becca's. I picked it up.

"Thanks, Stu."

I turned to find Becca behind me. "Oh, yeah. Here you go," I said, handing her the coat.

"What did you think?" she asked.

What did I think? I think Jackson should have his chin hair publicly plucked out by a giant, hair-sucking tarantula. "About what?"

Becca giggled. "About the dance? What did you think of the Spring dance?"

We walked toward the exit together.

"Oh, that. I thought it was okay. Except for the dancing. And the music. And pretty much everything else."

Becca dropped her chin and her voice. "I thought it was kind of fun. I thought jumping up and down was fun."

I wanted desperately to smack myself in the head. Why hadn't I said that? Was I stupid or just stupid? "Yeah, that's what I meant to say." It didn't come out at all convincing.

Becca waved and disappeared into the crowd.

Jackson came over and gave me a high five like we were a couple of sports stars meeting at midfield. "Hey, man, that was awesome!"

What would've been *awesome* would've been the disco ball dropping on his head right before he asked Becca to dance. "Yeah, awesome."

Jackson gave me a thumbs-up. "Excellent. That was an excellent dance."

Not as excellent as a poison dart sticking out of his butt cheek. "Excellent. Can't wait for the next one."

Jackson nodded in agreement. "No kidding. Did you slow-dance with anyone?"

I looked for our car. Where on earth was my

mother? If she didn't show up soon, I'd be forced to kill him with my bare hands. If only I had man hands. "No, not really."

"Too bad, it was pretty cool."

Thankfully, my mother arrived at that moment and motioned me over. "Gotta go," I said, wishing I could turn into the Hulk long enough to launch Jackson and his chin hair into space. Instead, I had to settle for a quiet ride home with my tiny, boyish hands held limply in my lap. One day, I'd have chin hair and man hands and the muscles to go with them. Please, God. Soon.

22

The next morning, I made a surprise visit to Ben's house.

"Get off me," he exclaimed as I tried to push his head through the mail slot in his front door.

I eased off the pressure on my knee that was planted firmly between his butt cheeks. "Where were you last night?" I yelled.

"It wasn't my fault," he sputtered through the mail slot. "My mother looked up my grades online."

"What part of your grades is not your fault?"

He twisted his head enough to pull his lips out of the slot. "It's not my fault my teachers posted grades the day of the dance."

"Why didn't you call me?"

"I did, but you'd already left."

"You suck."

Ben giggled. I yanked my knee out of his backside, and we both slumped down against the doorframe.

"How was it?"

The last song of the evening replayed in my mind. "It sucked, almost as much as you."

"C'mon, it couldn't have been that bad." He lowered his voice. "Was Kirsten there?"

"Yeah, she spent the evening with two really hot-looking guys."

Ben froze. My sentence had exactly the effect I was hoping for. He looked crushed.

"Who?" he said, almost too quietly.

"Me and Ryan," I said with a push. "I think she's pretty hot on Ryan."

Ben laughed a bit too loudly. "I should've known. He's huge, and he has chickens."

"It's all about the chickens," I agreed. "Talk about your chick magnet."

"I gotta get me some chickens."

"That's for darn sure. Something's gotta offset the size of your head."

"Shut up."

Clearly, everything was good between us once again. We spent the next two hours killing zombies until Ben's mom found us.

"I think you know better than to be playing video games this weekend," she said, giving him her stern stare.

"I know, I know. I was just being a good host."

She placed her hands on her hips. "Yes, I've never worried about you being a good host. However, I am worried about a few other things. Approximately six other things, none of which involve the letters A or B at the moment." She turned and left the room.

Ben's mom had a clever way of scolding him. I liked that about her. My mom was like that, too, except without the cleverness. Mostly, my mom got right to the point. I envied Ben.

"Looks like I better get to work," he said.

"I gotta get going anyway. Kirsten's waiting for me," I joked.

"Shut up."

I left Ben to stare down a pile of books larger than

his head, and that's saying something. After waving goodbye to his mom, I wandered down the sidewalk, feeling as if the world had been brought back into order once again. Ben was still Ben and we were back to being friends in a way I had relied on all my life. Life was good.

"Hey, Stu."

And then the Earth tilted. There she was standing right in front of me. No music, no friends around, and no Jackson. "Hi, Becca."

"How's Ben?"

My mouth went dry. The kind of dry that could kill a camel were one roaming on my tongue. "He's okay. His mom saw his grades online and kept him home. I think he's going to be there until the end of the year."

Becca shook her head. "That's too bad. Maybe he should try studying."

"Clearly, you don't know Ben."

Becca laughed. "I guess not." She looked back toward her house. "Hey, wanna try some zucchini bread my mom is baking?"

The idea of zucchini being put in bread was enough to make me swear off bread altogether. "Sure. Sounds good." My hands began to sweat. So did my armpits. Up until that moment, I'd never realized armpits could sweat so easily. Was this another fact of puberty? Evolution made no sense. How could armpit sweat have anything to do with survival of the fittest? Maybe survival of the wettest.

Becca led me up the front steps. At the top was a sitting porch with a love seat swing. Another round of dry mouth left me feeling like a salmon in the Sahara.

"Mom!" Becca called as she entered the house, "I've got a friend with me."

I stepped through the door into something that looked straight out of a magazine my mother would browse. There were gleaming hardwoods, gleaming white painted millwork, a gleaming chandelier, and a staircase that looked straight out of a Barbie playhouse. I had never seen anything so perfect in all my life. Not that I had spent much time looking, mind you. I nearly commented on the beauty of it all but, thankfully, caught myself before I sounded like a complete idiot. I confined myself to following Becca.

She led me into the kitchen, where her mother stood by the stove. Everything in the kitchen was white: the cabinets, the counters, the walls, and even her mother's apron. For a woman who seemed to do a lot of cooking, her apron looked perfectly pressed without a single stain anywhere. I wished I had taken time to shower that morning, or at least change my underwear. I felt like the lone spot of gravy on the Thanksgiving tablecloth. Hopefully I wouldn't leave a permanent stain.

"This is Stu," Becca said to her mother.

"Nice to meet you, Stu. Becca has told me all about you."

Becca stiffened. "Mom!"

Her mother ignored her and smiled pleasantly. "She tells me your family is vegetarian."

I felt my cheeks flush. Lying to Becca was one thing. Lying to her mother was a whole different matter. "Yes. We don't eat meat."

"How nice," her mother replied. "We went

vegetarian when Becca was just a baby. Has your family been vegetarian long?"

"No, not long." That much was true. As far as I knew, our transition to being vegetarian had begun just moments before. "We're still adjusting."

She pulled a loaf of something out of the oven. From the greenish color, it had to be the zucchini bread. "How's your dad doing with it? Becca's father had a hard time at first."

"He has his moments," I said.

Becca's mom pried the bread from the pan and sliced off three thick slices. She put the slices on a small plate, then passed it around so we could each take a piece.

"Mmm . . . that smells amazing," Becca said, holding her piece up to her nose.

I held up my piece, too, just far enough to realize a whiff of zucchini was enough of a treat for me. "Mmm . . . good," I said, trying not to let my nose wrinkle up in disgust.

"It's great warm with butter," Becca's mom said. "Would you like some?"

What I would like was a hole in the ground large

enough to return this thing to where it belonged. "No, thank you. This looks great just as it is."

Becca's mother picked up her piece. "Cheers," she said, taking a big bite.

"Cheers," Becca repeated, holding her piece up as if in toast.

"Cheers," I said, asking my stomach for forgiveness for what I was about to do. I took a bite. Memory of the roasted pepper sandwich returned to mind. "Could I get something to drink?" I mumbled through the zucchini paste stuck to my tongue.

"Of course, dear," Becca's mother said. She took a gleaming crystal glass and filled it full of gleaming white milk.

I gulped down the milk and the zucchini paste with it. "Wow, that was great," I lied with such earnestness I almost believed it myself.

Becca's mother beamed. "Yes, I got that impression. If you'd like I can give you the recipe for your mother."

I tried to imagine my family sharing such a treat. It would probably end with me left blindfolded in a back alley. "Yes, that would be great," I said politely.

Becca's mother refilled my glass. "Why don't you two finish eating on the porch. It's such a beautiful day. No need to stay cooped up in here."

Becca let out an audible sigh of relief. "Sounds good. Stu's helping me plan the sit-in at school that I was telling you about."

I am?

Becca's mother gave me a look. "She's not roping you in against your will, is she?"

Roping? No. Hog-tying? Maybe. "Oh, no. I think it's a great idea. It's about time the cafeteria added some food for us vegetarians."

"Entrées, he means," Becca chimed in. "They need to offer vegetarian entrées."

"Right," I agreed.

"Well, keep it courteous, whatever you do," Becca's mom said as she put the zucchini pan in the sink. "It's important to be courteous even when pushing for change."

"Yes, Mom." Becca rolled her eyes and pulled me out of the kitchen. "She's always so worried about being politically correct."

"Yeah, my mom, too."

Becca guided me back to the front door. On the way, I looked for a family pet in need of a zucchini treat. No such luck. Once outside, Becca headed over to the loveseat swing. "I've already got it pretty much planned out," she said, taking a seat.

Did she expect me to sit on the loveseat with her? I shifted from one foot to the other. I had never sat that close to a girl before. Doing so would be in plain sight of anyone passing by.

Becca giggled. She motioned to the empty seat beside her. "You don't have to stand."

I took a seat. The swing rocked slowly back and forth.

"I've got it all planned out. We're going to hold a sit-in. We'll take over the lunchroom and block the food service line. We can even give speeches. My dad has a megaphone he said we can use. I'm already making signs for us to hold," she continued excitedly. "We just need to pick a date and get everyone on board."

I nodded. The feeling of being exposed weighed on me almost as much as the zucchini bread in my lap.

Thank goodness Ben had a pile of homework that would keep him in his house until summertime. So long as Ben didn't happen by, everything would be okay.

"Hey, guys," Ben called from the street. "Whatcha doing?"

My stomach dropped.

Ben climbed the steps.

"We're having zucchini bread and finalizing the plan for the sit-in," Becca said, smiling.

I tried to give Ben my nothing-is-going-on-here look, but my face seemed frozen in more of a there-is-absolutely-something-going-on-here pose. Ben stood on the porch, eyeing me with a puzzled expression.

"Stu said you're in trouble."

Ben smiled. "Yeah, I can't leave the house until all my homework is done." He took the glass of milk out of my hand and drained the contents. He handed it back, being careful not to touch the zucchini bread. "They should know better than to send me to my room to work on it. We live in a one-story house."

Becca laughed. "So you're a fugitive?"

"Freedom fighter is the term I prefer."

I broke off a piece of the zucchini bread roughly the size of an elephant's head and idly stuffed it into my pocket. "Dumbhead is the term the rest of us use."

Ben leaned in. "I take it you made it to the dance?"

"Of course," Becca said, "decked out in black and everything. We missed you."

Ben tilted his head, still checking us out as if trying to determine whether we were aliens or something far more sinister. A light of recognition crossed his face. He immediately turned to go. "Well, I gotta get back before they notice I'm gone." He gave me a parting smile that said way more than I wanted to hear.

I stood. "Well, I gotta go, too. My mom needs help with something—or something like that," I stammered.

"Okay," Becca said, taking my glass and plate. "I guess we can pick a date at lunch on Monday."

"Sure. Sounds good."

She gave me a small wave, a look of disappointment on her face. Was she sad to see me go?

I paused for a moment, torn between my desire to stay and my desire to make it clear to Ben I wasn't at all interested in staying. "See ya," I said at last.

I headed down the steps.

"Stu?"

I turned to find Becca standing there. If I didn't know better I'd think her cheeks were flushed, just like mine.

"Yeah?"

She paused as if searching for just the right words. "Nothing," she said at last. "See you Monday." She gave me a last wave and then disappeared into the house.

23

At the end of the block, an arm pulled me into the bushes. Ben's face got in mine. "You dog!"

"What?" I said with all the innocence I could muster.

"You have a girlfriend!"

The force of the accusation was enough to knock me backward, that and Ben's breath. He needed to brush his teeth. "No, I don't," I pleaded.

He let go of me. "You liar. Why didn't you tell me?"

My head was spinning. "I'm not lying. We're not going out. I kinda like her, but—" I froze. What had I just said?

"I knew it! I knew you liked her!"

"No, I didn't mean I like her. I just meant—"

Ben stared at me expectantly.

"I just meant—" What did I mean? My shoulders slumped. "Shut up. And DO NOT tell anyone."

Ben grinned like an evil elf. "I knew it."

"Promise you won't tell anyone."

"Why would I tell anyone?"

"Because you're an evil elf."

"Shut up."

"You better not." It was time to bring out the big guns. "Because I know who *you* like, too."

"No, you don't."

"Kirsten."

You could have heard a pin drop, except that we were standing in the bushes on someone's lawn and it would have taken a pin packed with explosives to make a sound. I'd love to get my hand on some of those pins.

"So? Everybody knows that."

"Really? Then you won't mind if I call Tyler and Ryan when I get home and tell them?"

"You wouldn't."

"Wouldn't I? Remember the time you said everybody already knows your mom still warms your milk before bedtime?"

"Yeah, and they did know, but you lied and told them she gives it to me in a bottle." Ben stopped short. "What are you planning to tell them?"

I gave my best sinister smile. "Depends what *you* tell them."

"Oh, all right. I won't say anything."

"Then neither will I."

I held out my hand. Ben took it and we shook. Based on previous experience, this did little to comfort me. But what else could I do? If you can't trust your best friend to keep a secret, who can you trust? No one.

24

Monday in PE, Mr. Snedaker addressed the class. "I have some exciting news. This Friday is the all-school square dancing assembly."

A few, including Ben, clapped hands. The rest of us just murmured, "Finally." The assembly meant the end of the square dancing unit.

"I will be selecting the best dance partners," Mr. Snedaker continued, "to take part."

Fine by me. Given my skills, I felt confident my Friday afternoon would be spent comfortably watching from the safety of the bleachers. Gretchen seemed to be of the same opinion.

"That's unfair. What if I can dance but my partner can't?" she mumbled just loudly enough for me and everyone else to hear.

Ryan, Tyler, and I floated blissfully around the dance floor for the remainder of class, knowing the end was in sight. The only one of us who seemed at all disturbed by the news was Ben. He grumbled all the way to sixth period.

"Two weeks? What sort of unit is over in two weeks?"

"A unit that's already gone on two weeks too long," Tyler commented.

"And that was spawned by the devil," Ryan clarified.

"Go easy," I chimed in. "Can't you see he's upset? This has been the best two weeks of his life. You can imagine what the rest of it's been like."

"Shut up," Ben said. "Wouldn't you rather do this than health?"

"That question has already been answered," I corrected.

"Yeah," Tyler interjected, "how else you gonna know the difference between a uterus and a urinary tract?"

"That's right," I agreed. "Lives might be at stake!"

"Very funny," Ben said with a snarl that sounded like my dog when we try to wash his blanket.

"You're just sad because you won't get to hold

hands with Kirsten anymore," I let slip before I could stop myself.

That got him riled. "You're just sad because Jackson is partners with Becca and you're not," he snapped back.

You could have heard a pencil drop. Actually, a pencil did drop, the one Ryan had been holding. It landed on the sidewalk with a small *clunk*, next to Tyler's jaw.

Ben turned into the doorway of his class and disappeared without saying goodbye.

I kept my head down in the hopes neither Tyler nor Ryan had heard what they obviously had heard.

"You like Becca?" Ryan asked quietly.

I ignored the last comment and followed Tyler into class. He slipped off his backpack without looking up. "Girls are stupid," he mumbled before crossing to a desk against the far wall.

When class got underway, I tried to forget what had just happened by actually listening to Ms. Hendrickson, our science teacher, give a lecture on cell biology. She rambled on and on about all the wondrous parts to be discovered in a single cell. There was everything from walls to organs to a skeleton to a brain. When it came down to it, every cell was like a tiny person. And there were about 37 trillion of them in our bodies doing all the tasks necessary to keep us happy and healthy. I looked over at Tyler. Maybe he was short a few trillion cells. He looked healthy but not the least bit happy. Glancing around the room, I realized he wasn't alone. Everyone seemed to be short a few trillion cells. Not a happy face anywhere.

25

At dinner that evening, my father seemed in perfect cell health, smiling joyfully as he crunched the skin off his BBQ chicken.

"This is some fine chicken," he said, licking his lips.

My brother didn't seem to be on the same page. He gave his chicken leg one small lick and dropped it back on his plate. "Yuck. It's burned."

Reaching over, my father tore the skin off with his fingers. "Not to worry, chap. You're all good to go now."

You'd think my brother could remove something as simple as a piece of skin off his chicken without aid. Instead, he stared at the leg as if waiting for the meat to spontaneously pull itself off the bone, climb up his chest, and force its way into his mouth. My father chuckled as he went to work cutting the meat for him.

"What exactly is going on with you this evening?"

my mother asked.

"Nothing," my father replied. He gave a big, silly grin. "Can't a guy be helpful?"

She studied his face as if looking for a clue hidden behind his greasy lips. "No," she said flatly. "What's up?"

My father fed some chicken to my brother. "Nothing. I was just thinking that the festival starts next week. Should be a lot of fun." He gave me a wink.

"I hear there's going to be a big surprise," I added, trying to stir the pot.

"Is that so?" my mother said. "What sort of surprise?"

"I don't know. I'm hoping it involves explosions and a motorcycle stunt," I replied, hoping for a nod of agreement from my father.

"Don't you worry," my father said. "All will be revealed in due time. Just wait and see."

After dinner, my father pulled me aside. "Listen," he whispered. "I need you to tell Mom I had to run to the store for something."

"Why don't you tell her yourself?"

He gave me his that-woman-frightens-me look. "I need to slip out for a bit. Just tell her, okay?"

I couldn't really blame him. That woman frightened me, too. Plus, my father was a terrible liar. He tended to get his words all jumbled up, which usually ended with him saying exactly what he was trying to cover up. That was why he depended on me at times like this. I had a knack for telling the truth in a way that kept the truth safely hidden. It was a gift, really.

"Okay. What should I tell her you're running to the store for?"

"Just make something up," he encouraged.

"Like wet wipes?"

"No. What would I need wet wipes for?"

"I don't know. I'm just trying to think of something you might get at the store."

"Say something a man would get."

"Like cigars?"

"No! You don't buy cigars at the grocery store."

"You didn't say you were going to the grocery store. Can't you just get what you need tomorrow?"

My father let out an exasperated groan. "Just make something up, okay?"

"Okay, how about deodorant?"

My father opened the garage door like a clumsy burglar. "Yes, that's fine," he said disappearing into the night.

I went into the kitchen. "Mom, Dad ran to the store to get some deodorant."

It was my turn to get a look from her. "What is he really up to?"

"I don't know."

My mother bent until her face was right in mine. "Be honest. Do you know what he's really doing?"

Hmm . . . how far was he expecting me to go in covering for him? "I don't know. Maybe it has to do with that trailer." That was only giving away what she probably already knew.

My mother rolled her eyes. "That's what concerns me." She leaned against the counter. "If you find out what's going on, tell me. Okay?"

I nodded like the good son I was. "Of course." That last line might have been a bit over the top, but what's a guy to do when he knows his father is building a secret parade float and sewing some sort of nylon bodysuits? Yikes.

Just before bed, the phone rang. "Stu, it's Ben," my mom called.

I answered the phone with my politest be-glad-you're-not-here-or-I'd-be-riding-your-fat-head-like-a-rodeo-clown voice. "What do you want?"

"You're a jerk."

Seriously? "You're the jerk."

"You gonna tell Ryan and Tyler that, too?"

"Shut up, or while I'm at it, I'll tell them you still wear Aquaman undies to bed."

"They're summer jammies, and they've already seen them. And anyways, I only wear them because they're silky smooth."

He had a point. "True, they are silky smooth."

"Why'd you open your big mouth?" His voice sounded more hurt than angry.

"I don't know. Why'd you?"

"Man, you can't keep anything secret."

If only he knew. "Like you can?"

That brought a giggle. "Did you see Tyler? I thought he was gonna choke on his own tongue. Did you hear him gulping for air?"

"Ryan looked like he was gonna puke."

"That kid pukes a lot. Remember first grade?"

"Yeah, I still can't go near Chinese food."

"Me neither. Did you finish the math homework?"

"No. You?"

"Nope. But at least I did the history assignment."

"Oh crud, is it due tomorrow?"

"Yeah, that's why she wrote *DUE TOMORROW* on the whiteboard."

"Shut up. I gotta go."

"See you tomorrow."

"See you."

The phone hung up with a click. Ben could be a total doofus, but he wasn't one to hold a grudge. Lucky for him because otherwise I would have ridden his head like a rodeo clown for real.

With that out of the way, I could focus on more pressing things. Like a four-paragraph paper to finish before bed. How did the Incas impact modern civilization? I headed upstairs. It was going to be a long ten minutes.

26

Thursday afternoon took way too long to arrive. Getting there required enduring three more days of square dancing with a partner bordering on criminally insane. Gretchen had taken to stepping on my toes for no apparent reason. Yes, there may have been moments I was caught daydreaming. Yes, there may have been a lot of those moments. Okay, maybe every moment seemed better spent staring into space than listening to the same song for the millionth time.

"Pay attention," Gretchen commanded, pirouetting on my toe like a demon ballerina.

"Ow!" I shouted. "I'm trying."

She pulled me back to the correct group. I had apparently strayed while dozing. "No, you're not."

To my right, Tyler was attempting to tie his shoe.

He had been working on his laces for three days. From the looks of it, he was in need of a cobbler's bench and a surgical nurse. Dang, why hadn't I thought to tangle my laces? That kind of ingenuity doesn't get the respect it deserves. To my left, Ryan was ducking and dodging for all he was worth to avoid being sucked into the vortex known as Debbie's armpit. She kept yanking him along like a rag doll. To his credit, he had hung in there a lot longer than any of the rest of us would have.

In the distance, I caught sight of Ben and Kirsten prancing about like a pair of circus ponies, all smiles and leg kicks no matter how stupid they looked.

Across from them, Jackson and Becca tucked and turned as if they had been dancing together since birth. His lone chin hair gleamed in the fluorescent lighting next to her perfectly aligned teeth. I dreamed of pulling that hair out at long last and shoving it up his—

"Ow! Now what?" I exclaimed.

Gretchen pulled the heel of her boot off the top of my foot, ignoring the crater she left behind. "Pay attention!" she bellowed.

A few moments later, Ben and Kirsten came prancing

by, followed by Becca and Jackson. Both couples appeared to have gone AWOL from their group. The two couples twirled their way over to where Mr. Snedaker was standing. He pointed to two more couples and motioned for them to join the group. Strangely, he didn't look in my direction at any time. You'd think Gretchen jumping up and down like a pogo stick on my right toe yelling, "PAY ATTENTION!" would at least have garnered a glance.

The music ended. Finally. That annoying fiddle-ridden song bound to haunt me into old age. If I happened across that fiddler in real life, he'd better have sprinter speed or a cloaking device. He'd need it.

Mr. Snedaker waved the class over. "I'm pleased to present the representatives from your class for the assembly tomorrow."

A murmur of approval went up.

"I'm sure they will do great, and I know they will have your full support as they perform." He looked about with a pleasantly evil stare. "Don't forget—your performance as an audience will be graded."

I wanted to ask more about his grading scale, but

the timing didn't seem right. I was pretty sure pointing and laughing wouldn't earn an A, but what about a discreet chuckle? Or a soft snore?

Tyler poked my side. "Can you believe it?" he whispered. "It's over."

Ryan yanked his head out of Debbie's armpit and leaned in. "Look at those suckers," he said, pointing at the chosen few.

The comment would have been funnier had the couples looked at all disappointed with their selection. On the contrary, they looked way too pleased with themselves. There should be a law against that sort of self-congratulatory behavior. Especially the hugging. The last thing I needed to see was hugging at a time like this. "Yeah, look at the disappointment on their faces."

"Just wait until tomorrow," Tyler said. "We'll see who's laughing when they have to get up in front of the whole school."

Yeah, just think of that. Becca and Jackson holding hands in front of the whole school. Who'll have the last laugh then?

27

That night at dinner, I did my best to keep my feelings of frustration secret.

"He just took my piece of steak!" my little brother yelled, for absolutely no reason.

"Stu, give your brother back his steak."

My mother was quick to take sides. I bit off most of the piece and dumped what was left back onto my brother's plate.

"He ate it!" Tommy hollered.

"Not all of it," I corrected.

"He ate the good part!"

"The good part is that I didn't eat it *all*," I corrected again. Geesh, the kid made no sense at all.

My mother set down her fork. "Stuart Cornelius Truly! What has gotten into you? Do I need to have you move to the kitchen and eat by yourself?"

That seemed like an excellent idea. I rose with my plate.

"Bill, do something here," my mother snapped.

"Stu, sit down. Don't eat your brother's meat," my father said, without looking up from the construction site on his plate. His steak and potatoes were stacked together with a roll on top that looked a little like a snack shack or an outhouse depending on what the butter and blackberry jam were doing inside.

I sat back down.

"What would you think of us doing a family hike Sunday?" my mother asked, rubbing her temples.

My father looked up, startled. "Sunday? Can't. Gotta work Sunday."

My mother set down her fork again. I could see her nostrils opening and closing like an angry bull. "Bill, what exactly are—" She stopped, then stared down at her plate as she bit her lip.

"What's that?" my father asked.

"Nothing," my mother replied after a long pause. "Nothing, I hope."

28

The next morning started off with the sort of surprise that is usually reserved for movies. Not good movies, mind you. I mean the kind where the heroine, through some sort of impossible coincidence, becomes queen of a small European nation inhabited with whimsical folk all too willing to be captivated by her winning charm. This is not the sort of movie I watch except when spending an evening with my mother doing "something we'll both enjoy." Those are the moments when I realize my mother needs a daughter, or a happy-go-lucky mouse child.

I was almost to my first-period class when things took a rather HUGE turn.

"Stu!" Becca called, waving at me.

"Hi, Becca," I said, wishing I had borrowed my father's deodorant that morning instead of splashing cold water under my pits and calling it good.

"I need your help!"

"Sure. Okay."

Becca beamed. "Jackson is sick and had to stay home from school today."

A sharp pain jabbed me in the stomach. I didn't like where this was going.

"Would you be my dance partner for the assembly?"

Say what? My knees quivered. One foot tried to make a break for it but was held back by my ankle. Had she seen me dance? "Sure."

That was not a well-thought-out response. I immediately attempted to take the statement back, but my lips had crawled down my throat and were working to free my foot from my ankle so the three of them could secede from the union of my body parts.

"Awesome!" Becca said as she reached out and hugged me. That's right. H-U-G-G-E-D M-E.

This was the first time I had ever been hugged by a

girl. It was a moment that should have been captured on film. Or at least in an epic poem. I didn't have time for either.

"I'll see you this afternoon," she said, pulling away.

"Okay. See you," I replied, wondering what had just happened.

Becca skipped away as if the thought of square dancing was enough to make her want to dance. I stared down at my own feet frozen in place like two blocks of sneakered wood. They did not look like dancer's feet. More like baby elephant feet, which was ironic since I had the body of a stick bug. If there's one thing I know, it's that a stick bug with elephant feet should not be dancing in public. Especially if the public consists of your friends.

The rest of the morning passed in a blur of confusion, fear, and guilt. The confusion was over whether it was too late to change my name to Armando and move east of the Rockies. The fear was pretty self-explanatory. And the guilt was over how much joy I got from the fact Jackson was home sick. Let's be honest, were it up to me, he'd also be suffering from an acute foot fungus and a severe case of muscle sag, especially in the bicep region. But we don't get everything we want in life.

At lunch, I was forced to listen to Ben, Kirsten, and Becca jabber away about how cool the assembly was going to be.

"I heard there's a competition," Kirsten bubbled out.

"Yeah, with a winner and everything," Ben added, a gleeful look in his eye.

"Sounds like fun," Becca shrieked with excitement.

Boy, howdy, did it ever. What could possibly be more fun than being judged on how well you do-si-do in front of your peers? With luck, there'd be a hog-calling contest and a greased pig to chase up the bleachers, too.

"I wish they did an all-school dance, like an old-fashioned hoedown," Kirsten said, clapping her hands together like a little girl.

Ben clapped his hands in return, also looking like a little girl. "That would be cool."

Whatever was possessing my best friend, I hoped a priest could exorcise it. Though from the silly grin on his face, it didn't look likely. That demon seemed set on staying.

"I feel bad for Jackson," Becca said. "He's missing out." She looked at me. "Although, I'm happy you get to join us."

Lucky me. I was beginning to envy Jackson again. He'd spent the last two weeks holding Becca's hand and then had the good fortune to be at home with a fever the day of the assembly. How lucky can one guy get? "Yeah, I'm happy, too."

By the end of lunch, the pit in my stomach had grown large enough to start a mining operation. I walked to the gym like an inmate on death row after his last meal. Lethal injection sounded like a party compared to what I had ahead of me. The gym was already filling up. I didn't remember there being so many kids at our school. I began to wonder if other middle schoolers had been bused in just to intimidate the dancers. If so, it was working splendidly. Ben ran up from behind and punched me in the shoulder.

"It's go time."

Yes, I was more than willing to go, the farther away the better. Tibet beckoned. In fact, this seemed like a perfect time for my first space walk.

Ben dragged me over to where Mr. Snedaker was waiting. The other dancers milled about, chatting in excited whispers. Where he had found such an energetic, compliant group was beyond me. The least they could do was show a little taste and bemoan this obvious example of student abuse. Instead, they seemed to be enjoying the attention being lavished upon them by their teacher.

"I'm so excited for all of you," Mr. Snedaker said. "You are the best of the best." He eyed me with one raised eyebrow. "I know you're going to do great today. Best of luck to you all."

"He's so nice," Becca whispered, stepping beside me.

She smelled of perfume. Maybe she always did, but at that moment, the subtle sweetness enveloped me like a warm mist. It was as if a spell had been cast over me from some fairy tale. I would have followed Becca anywhere. Which is exactly what I did. What other explanation could there be for why I walked unaided to the middle of the gym?

We broke into groups, just like we had been rehearsing for the last two weeks. Instinctively, I curled my big toes to avoid having them jackhammered into the floor. Becca took my hand. My toes relaxed. Their days of abuse were over. Holding Becca's hand wasn't so bad, either. Maybe this wasn't going to be so awful after all. And then the music started.

Suddenly, I regretted not having paid closer attention in class. I seemed to be a half step behind at every turn. This meant hurrying after Becca while trying to maintain my manly cool. Somewhere between "take your partner by the hand" and "turn your partner 'round and 'round," my manly cool got permanently lost. By "do-si-do," I was sweating like a prizefighter. And then came the complicated part of the dance. Everyone moved every which way all at once, fanning out to form a circle around the center of the dance floor. I spun, looking for Becca, but she had disappeared on the far side of the circle.

The truth dawned on me. We were the lead couple for the finale. Becca had told me so earlier, but I had been too preoccupied with the smell of her perfume for the news to register. It registered now. At the prescribed moment, we were to enter the circle from opposite sides and come together in the middle for a twirling finish.

Someone glared at me. I had missed my cue. I burst through the ring of dancers hoping to God I wasn't too late in making my grand entrance. My foot caught on someone's shoe. I stumbled forward, my momentum sending me right into the back of Becca's spinning head. I heard a crunching sound followed by a series of gasps from the other dancers. I looked down to see blood gushing from my nose, much of which was running down the back of her sweater. "Oh my God!" someone screamed. The music stopped.

Ben rushed over and checked out my face. "Dude, that's nasty."

I seemed to have lost all feeling in my body. I stared blankly about as Ben ushered me to the boys' bathroom. In the mirror, I saw something that looked like a bloodthirsty monster dripping after a kill, except the blood was my own. On the other side of the wall, I heard Becca sobbing in the girls' room.

Mr. Snedaker rushed in. "Are you all right?"

"I've been better," I said, holding a wad of tissue to my nose.

"Let's get you to the nurse," he said, guiding me by the elbow.

The nurse took one look and gave her diagnosis: "Your nose is broken."

Sure, my nose now took a right-hand turn where there used to be a straightaway, but didn't that happen to everyone square dancing? According to her, no.

"Your parents will need to take you to the doctor," she explained, mopping up after me.

I had experienced that sort of *fixing* before. It was going to be a long, ugly afternoon. "Is Becca okay?"

"She's in with the vice principal until her mom arrives," the nurse explained. "She's got a bit of a goose egg on the back of her head, but other than that, nothing a little shampoo and detergent can't get out."

My mom arrived and gave me a hug. "School has been a dangerous place for you this spring. Anything going on I should know about?"

Not really. Other than a new girl being responsible for our second trip to the doctor. Maybe there would be a right time to share that news, like on my deathbed. "No. Just unlucky, I guess."

29

The visit to the doctor's office went well, if you consider getting your nose reset without anesthesia a good time. Fortunately, I saw the same doctor as on my previous visit.

"You look familiar," he said. "Didn't you get into an altercation with a stapler a few weeks ago?"

He seemed to think that was a funny remark. I might have agreed, if my nose wasn't rubbing against my right ear.

"Here we go," he said, gripping the flap of skin formerly known as my nose. He proceeded to pull my nose down to my belly button and then snapped it back into place like a clown tying a balloon animal.

By the time I got home, my screams had subsided

to gentle sobs, and if you ignored all the swelling, you might have thought I'd been in nothing more than a barroom brawl. That was a real improvement.

"I'd hate to see what the other guy looks like," my father said when he got home that evening.

"The other guy was a girl, and it was an accident," my mother explained.

"An accident? What were they doing? Cage fighting?"

"Dancing."

My father gave me a puzzled look. "Dancing has changed a lot since I was your age."

I spent the rest of the evening in my room trying to forge a passport to get out of the country while practicing my new name. Armando. My name is Armando. I sure the heck wasn't going back to school. My mother must have sensed my anxiety. She stopped by before bed to check on me.

"I'm sure everyone will have forgotten by Monday," she said.

"No, they won't."

"Honey, just be patient. It was just an accident. It's going to be okay."

She stroked the top of my head. I refused to acknowledge that it made me feel better, even though it did.

"It must've been very traumatic for that poor girl."

The last image of Becca flashed to mind. She had looked as if she had been pelted with tomatoes, only it wasn't tomato juice running down the back of her head and splattered all over her sweater. It reminded me of the night Ben and I stayed up and watched the end of the movie *Carrie*.

"How about instead of feeling sorry for yourself, you do something nice for her?"

That sounded like about the dumbest idea ever. "Uh, like what?"

"Maybe you could take her some flowers." She kissed me on the head and headed for the door. "Think about it."

That night, I tried to imagine the cabin in the woods and Becca in need of rescuing but, try as I might, I couldn't imagine any scenario in which I would ever again be Becca's hero. Instead of defeating zombies, I had become one of them. Every time I came to her aid, my nose would turn sideways or one of my arms would fall off and Becca would run screaming.

30

I woke exhausted. And my nostrils still looked the size of my butt cheeks. I stared into the bathroom mirror and saw a beastly creature staring back at me with two black eyes and enough puffiness to fill a pastry. I consoled myself that I probably didn't look as bad to others as I did to myself.

"AHH!!!" my little brother screamed in the hallway.

Then again, maybe I did.

After breakfast, I contemplated my options. Hide in my room until I grew old and died. Or take Becca flowers on the off chance the sight of me didn't make her physically ill. Hiding until I died of old age seemed the better choice. Instead, I went out back and set to picking flowers from my mother's garden. My mother, whom I'm pretty sure had been lying in wait, joined me.

"Those are excellent choices," she said, replacing the handful I'd picked with a dazzling variety she seemed to pull out of thin air. "Is she a nice girl?"

That was a loaded question if I'd ever heard one. "She's okay," I offered noncommittally.

"I see. I don't suppose you're going to invite me along when you take these to her?"

I'd rather straighten my own broken nose than risk showing up on Becca's doorstep with my mother in tow. "I think I can do this on my own."

She stared up at me as if seeing me for the first time. "You're growing up," she said quietly. "I'm going to have to get used to that."

She motioned toward the gate. "Well, you better be off. Those flowers will need to be put in water soon."

I set out at a leisurely pace that I hoped would take roughly forty-five years to complete. With luck, Becca would have moved away and forgotten all about me by the time I arrived. Unfortunately, even with dragging my feet, I found myself at the bottom of her steps far too soon. The idea passed through my mind that I could bypass her house, and saunter on down to Ben's instead. Normally, the idea of spending a couple hours playing *Death Intruders 4* would have been pretty irresistible. But today I had no interest in seeing blood, even the digital kind that looked more like day-old ketchup.

Facing Ben would have presented its own set of problems. For one thing, I would never again be able to tease him about the size of his head without being reminded of my current resemblance to a blowfish. And God only knew what sort of trivia it would bring to mind. He probably had read about a guy who had broken his nose 432 times or who had once drained all the blood from his own body, then poured it back in using a funnel and a garden hose. This was not the sort of cheering up I needed at the moment. Going to Becca's wasn't exactly cheery either, yet I was drawn there like a moth to the proverbial flame, despite knowing how that usually ends.

An elderly man passed by as I tried to find the courage to climb the steps. He studied the flowers in my hand and the expression of fear pasted on my face.

"Good luck," he said with a wink.

I wanted to clarify that I was not engaged in some sort of old-fashioned courting ritual. But I suddenly wasn't so sure. What exactly was I doing? I was about to knock on a girl's front door with a bouquet of flowers. Yes, I was coming to apologize. Yes, I was checking to make sure she was okay. But I sure as heck wouldn't be bringing flowers if it were anyone else. How had I let my mother talk me into this? Panic set in. The zombie warlord started pounding inside my chest again.

I willed myself up the steps and knocked on the front door. From the other side, footsteps approached, heavy footsteps. The door opened, and I found myself face-to-face with Becca's father.

"Can I help you?" he said in a voice so low it sounded like the rumble of Harley's motorcycle.

The zombie warlord in my chest stopped in

midhammer. My tongue went so dry it felt like a bucket of sand. "Uh—uh," I stammered. "I came by to see Becca."

He looked down at the flowers I was holding in my spaghetti-string arms, then up at my misshapen nose surrounded by two black eyes. From his viewpoint, I looked like a praying mantis crossed with a raccoon. At last, he let out a slow breath and turned.

"Becca," he called up the stairs, "there's someone here to see you." He turned back and gave me a final once-over as if hoping someone more acceptable might have replaced me while his back was turned. We both knew better.

Becca came bouncing down the stairs looking like an angel descending from heaven, her golden hair bouncing in perfect waves over her shoulders. There appeared to be no sign of blood anywhere on her. I breathed a small sigh of relief.

"Stu," she said, a smile lighting up her face.

"You know this boy?" her father asked.

Becca giggled. "Yeah, of course. He's the one that

accidentally ran into me yesterday while we were dancing."

I held up the flowers. "I'm sorry about what happened. I didn't mean to gush blood all over you."

Becca took the flowers. "Stu, that's so nice of you, but you didn't need to bring me flowers."

"My mother made me," I said too quickly.

Becca's father smirked as he moved out of the way. Becca stepped onto the porch and closed the door behind her. "Are you okay?" she asked, staring at the swollen mass formerly known as my face.

"Yeah," I replied, trying to sound tough. "My nose got broken, but it's doing okay now."

Becca winced. "That must have really hurt."

"Not as much as all the scrubbing you must've endured to get your hair clean," I said.

"You have no idea," she said with a laugh. "It was pretty gross." She looked at my face more closely. "I'm so sorry about what happened."

The sincerity in her voice moved through me like hot cocoa. "It was my fault. I jumped into the circle at the wrong time. I'm a terrible dancer."

"No, you're not," she said. "Well, maybe a little."

We both giggled.

"If I was only a little terrible, my head wouldn't be swollen larger than Ben's right now."

"That's not fair," she said. "Your head's not *that* swollen."

That girl knew how to be funny.

"Thank you. That makes me feel better."

Becca showed me the notepad she was holding. "I was just talking to Kirsten. We've set the date of the sit-in for the Friday after the Irrigation Festival Parade. Kirsten says we should wait until the festival is over. She thinks maybe the paper will run a story on us since that's usually a slow news week."

"Sure. Sounds good." The mere fact she was talking to me sounded good. Right at that moment, I would have agreed to anything just to see an excited smile on her face.

"That's awesome. I can't wait!"

I could wait, but there was no need dwelling on that now. "Yeah, me too."

A rumbling sound came from down the street, growing louder as a motorcycle came into view. The motorcycle stopped in front of Becca's house. Harley waved.

"Hey, Stu," he called. "Your dad is trying to track you down."

"That's my dad's friend, Harley," I explained to Becca. "They go way back." I waved at Harley. "What does he want?"

Harley switched off the engine on his bike. "He wants to show you something. I was on my way to Ben's house looking for you." He looked at the flowers in Becca's hands. A grin spread from ear to ear. "I see you didn't make it that far."

The little part of my face that wasn't swollen turned a deep shade of red. Why does everyone jump to the conclusion if you're standing next to a girl holding flowers that something is going on?

"Hey, if you're busy, I can come back for you later."

The whole situation suddenly felt out of hand. It wasn't what it looked like. Or was it? "No, that's okay," I called back. I turned to Becca. "Looks like I gotta go."

"Thanks for stopping by," she said. "The flowers are beautiful."

"I'm sorry again for bleeding all over you yesterday."

She smiled. "See you later."

"See you." I hurried down the steps, forcing myself not to look back. My mother was a genius. Never again would I ignore her advice.

Harley gave me a nod of approval. "Nice," he said. "That girl's cute."

My cheeks burned. I tried to make a witty reply but all that came out was a gurgling sound.

Harley gave me a bump with his elbow. "Been there, man." He started his bike, then handed me a helmet and motioned for me to climb on behind him.

"My mother won't let me ride on your bike."

"Don't worry," Harley replied. "Your father said you'd say that. He's giving you one-time permission to ride with me." He leaned close. "Just don't tell your mother, okay?"

I grinned as I pulled on the helmet. "No problem."

My first ride on a motorcycle would have been a lot

more exciting if I hadn't been sitting behind someone the size of the Jolly Green Giant. My view was limited to Harley's leather jacket and whatever whizzed past my peripheral vision. Since we were traveling at roughly the speed of light, I wasn't able to identify much. It didn't help matters that the windchill kept dropping below zero despite it being a balmy spring day. A coat would have been a real help. I concentrated on sending blood flow to my fingers in the hope they wouldn't snap off before we got there.

Finally, after what seemed like hours but was probably not more than twenty minutes, we pulled into Harley's farm. When I say farm, I mean a collection of buildings that at one time, probably shortly before the Civil War, had been used as a farm. Since then, they had been let go and appeared to be slowly returning to their natural state. The front porch had long ago separated from the main house and looked to be hitchhiking its way across the front lawn. The only building still holding up on its own was the barn. It sported a new roof and corrugated metal siding that looked downright modern. I couldn't blame Harley for spending his money where it mattered most, the building that housed his motorcycle.

We rode up to the barn, and Harley shut off the engine. I climbed off and set to work massaging circulation back into the pile of goose bumps my body had become. My father hurried out of the barn with a grin the size of Harley's mustache.

"You're here!" he exclaimed.

His excitement, combined with the mysterious motorcycle ride, gave me the sneaking suspicion that whatever they were working on in the barn, I didn't want to know about.

"Wait till you see what we've been up to," he said, ushering me toward the barn door.

I could wait, really. Unless it was a warm blanket. My body still felt numb with cold from the ride.

As we drew near, my father stopped. He placed his hands on my shoulders.

"What you're about to see is top secret. Understand? You can't tell a soul, especially your mother."

My instincts told me to run before it was too late.
"Okay."

With a flourish, my father pulled open the barn door. The interior was too dark for me to see anything. Cautiously, I stepped inside. As my eyes adjusted to the dim light, I recognized the trailer. But what exactly they had done with it I couldn't tell.

"Behold," my father said with the voice of a true showman. He flipped on the overhead lights.

I let out a gasp, not of awe, mind you. Before me stood a creation that looked like a child's art project gone awry. I walked in a circle around the trailer trying to make sense out of what I was seeing. Scraps of old lumber, outdoor carpet, butcher paper, and a host of metal implements had been thrown together into what looked like a mobile torture chamber.

"Uh, what is it?" I asked.

"What is it, you say?" my father motioned like a game show host. "What is it? It's a monument to what has made our family great."

To be honest, the creation before me was doing little for my family pride.

He climbed onto the trailer and lifted his arms like

a traveling evangelist. "What you see here is a parade float that brings together the past and the present. For three generations, the Truly name has stood for one thing—MEAT!" He stared out into the darkness, his arms still raised, like Zeus about to call lightning down from the heavens.

"It's a meat float?" I asked.

My father stared down at me, looking a bit deflated. "Yes, that's what I just said." He raised his arms again, though without the same vigor. It was as if I had pricked a tiny pinhole in his balloon and the air was slowly leaking out. "Don't you see? We've re-created the original Truly butcher shop." He pointed to the implements hanging about. "See? These are meat hooks. Over here is a replica of my grandfather's chopping block. And this here is the actual bucket he used for draining blood."

My stomach began to churn, not just from the horror, but from the thought that my father believed he had created something spectacular. "Dad, you're not actually going to enter this in the parade, are you?"

If my father had appeared to be leaking air before, he was spewing it out now like an untied balloon. "Of course we're going to enter it in the parade! The town is filled with old-timers. They're going to love it." He hopped down off the float and pulled a box from underneath. "You haven't even seen the best part yet." He lifted out what looked like a giant rib cage wearing women's stockings. "This is your costume," he said proudly.

I backed away. Whatever it was, it didn't look dead yet. "What is that?"

My father forced the costume into my hands. "Weren't you listening? It's your costume. We're all dressing up like a favorite cut of meat. You're a half rack of ribs."

My father had lost his mind. How could grown men have built something so crazy without anyone stating the obvious?

"I'm not wearing this," I said, mimicking my mother's eye roll.

"What do you mean?" my father shouted. "I thought you liked meat!"

"I do," I shouted back. "I just don't want to BE a piece of meat."

Harley came up beside me. "No need to get yourself too worked up, little dude."

I turned to find him in a costume that made him look like a three-hundred-pound ham hock. I had to admit seeing him that way was pretty darn funny.

"You're seriously going to wear that in the parade?"

"People are going to love it." He had a grin on his face that was irresistible. "And it's going to give Truly Meats all the publicity your dad needs right now."

I laughed, despite the voice in the back of my head warning me this would not end well.

"C'mon," my father said, "you gotta admit we're going to steal the show at this year's parade."

I looked again at Harley in his ham hock suit, then at the costume spilling over in my hands.

"Wait till you see this," my father said. He held up what looked like a sixty-pound drumstick. "This is what your brother is going to wear."

The idea of my brother dressed like a drumstick with the bone sticking out his butt brought a whole new dimension to the idea.

"You don't want to miss out on this crazy ship, do you?" Harley asked.

"Couldn't he be a fried chicken gizzard?" I threw out.

Harley and my father laughed. "No," my father said. "Maybe next year."

I held my costume up to get a better look. There were worse things than being a half rack of ribs. Like being a chicken leg, for instance. Or a ham hock. "What are you going to be?" I asked my father.

"Ah," he said with a twinkle in his eye, "I still have a few surprises up my sleeve. You'll see soon enough. You'll see."

32

By the time I got home, I had almost convinced myself the meat float was a good idea. After all, how often did you get a chance to dress up in a short rib costume and ride through town with your father's friends? Maybe they were right. Maybe we would be the hit of the parade.

I entered the kitchen to find my mother holding a paper plate wrapped in plastic.

"A young lady stopped by with this for you," she said with a smile far too pleased for my own good.

"What is it?" I asked.

She pulled the plastic wrap back to reveal a lovely loaf of zucchini bread. "According to her, this is your favorite."

"Um, yeah . . . well, about that—" What exactly was I ready to reveal to my Mom? "I hate zucchini bread."

"Well, at least I know it's my son I'm talking to and not an alien. She seemed like a very nice girl. She also said to tell you thanks again for the flowers. I take it she's the one you were dancing with yesterday?"

My mom was pretty quick with the obvious. Apparently, I had not inherited that trait from her. The reality that Becca would see me on the parade float washed over me like a BBQ sauce tsunami. How could I have overlooked that obvious fact?

"Yeah, she's the one."

"I see," my mother said. "Well, I thought she was lovely. It was nice meeting her."

I retreated to my room. Becca thought I was vegetarian. In one week, I'd be riding on a float proclaiming a love of meat that went back generations in my family. What was I going to do? I couldn't disappoint my father, not after what had just gone down in Harley's barn. But I couldn't go through with it, either. The whole situation had spiraled out of control.

At the moment, what I needed was a way to clear

my head. A way to ignore my problems and focus on something simple, something I could grasp, something real. I headed for Ben's house. *Death Intruders 4* was exactly what I needed. Sure, maybe the idea of blood had grossed me out this morning, but so much had happened since then. A little fake blood seemed like nothing to me now. And more than anything, I craved being a child even if only for a little while.

Ben waited at the door for me when I arrived. Sometimes it seemed as if we had a telepathic connection between us.

"I saw you coming down the street," he said.

Okay, maybe not telepathic but at least he had good vision.

"I need to kill some zombies," I replied.

"I'm with you there, dude." He stared at my swollen face. "I just hope you're not becoming one of them."

"Shut up."

We spent the next two hours in zombie wedded bliss. I say that because at one point on level twenty-two we were forced to marry zombie brides, who then chased us with chain saws on our honeymoon. If marriage in real life was anything like that, Ben and I would be married already, maybe twice. After a quick lunch of Cheetos and Otter Pops, we relaxed back on the couch in the family room and put our feet up.

"Your shoes are the size of dog sleds," Ben said with admiration.

"Thank you. Comes in handy in the winter."

"I wish I had big feet. I look like a hamster when I walk."

"Don't worry, your head more than compensates."

"Shut up. Have you looked in the mirror lately?"

"Yeah, unfortunately."

Ben took a closer look. "That must have really hurt."

"Pretty much. I'm hanging up my square dancing shoes."

"Can't blame you. It was pretty fun, though."

"Maybe for you. I've gotta have one of my toes grafted back on. Gretchen ground it off."

"That'd be pretty cool. I read about a guy who lost all his fingers. They grafted some of his toes onto his hands. He could write and drive and everything."

"I wonder what happens when he taps his feet."

"Shut up." Ben turned suddenly serious. "Kirsten wants to go to the carnival Friday night. She wants you and Becca to come with us."

Every year during the Irrigation Festival, a cheesy carnival comes to town. It's the sort of carnival that travels from backwater hole to backwater hole. Some of the rides are so old you can find your parents' initials carved on them next to their parents' initials. There are also a host of games guaranteed to defy the laws of physics and cheat you out of your hard-earned allowance. This was not to say I didn't enjoy going to the carnival. On the contrary, the flashing lights, cotton candy smells, and screams that fill the air are a break from the humdrum of normal small-town life. Except for one small problem.

"I can't go with Becca."

Ben stopped cold. "What do you mean?"

The image of me in a half rack of ribs suit sprang to mind.

"She thinks I'm vegetarian."

"She what? Doesn't she know your dad owns the butcher shop?"

I let my shoulders sag. "No, and that's the problem. My dad is planning a float for the parade to promote his business. He wants me to ride on the float. She's going to see me."

Ben fought to control the giggles rippling through his body. "Dude. You're screwed."

I politely shoved him to the floor. "It's not funny. She's gonna kill me."

Falling to the floor did little to stop Ben's giggles. He curled up like a giggling snake. "Dude, why did you tell her you were vegetarian?"

That guy knew how to get right to the heart of the matter. If only he had a heart.

I slumped against the doorframe. "Because I'm an idiot. Sometimes I say things around her for no reason."

Ben stiffened. "Yeah, I know what you mean. Kirsten told me she sometimes listens to Christie Moreno and I said I did, too."

I smirked loud enough to wake Ben's cat. "You what?"

"I know. It just came out."

I pulled him to his feet. "At least you don't have to dress up in a Christie Moreno outfit for the parade."

"True," he agreed.

"No point going to the carnival with you guys. Once she finds out, there's no way she'll agree to go with me."

Ben paused in thought. "I think you're forgetting something."

"What's that?"

"The carnival is the night *before* the parade. She won't know yet."

Hmm . . . his logic did have something to it. "I don't know. I'm not sure I can live the lie any longer."

"C'mon," Ben begged, "it's just for a few more days. It'll be fun."

I pointed to my nose. "You mean square dancing fun?"

"No. Better. C'mon."

What could be better than square dancing fun? I guess there was only one way to find out. "Oh, alright."

33

Monday, I stood in the doorway to the lunch room with my brain in full-scale turmoil. Jackson was back and already seated next to Becca. Tyler and Ryan were eyeing me like two lost puppy dogs in need of a pat on the head. And I had the sneaking suspicion that everyone else was staring at my swollen face. I had that sneaking suspicion because everyone all morning had been staring at my face. I couldn't blame them. It's not often you see a real-life zombie walking around school.

I shuffled toward Tyler and Ryan. Before I got more than a couple steps, hands waved at me from the opposite direction. Ben and Kirsten motioned for me to join them. Abruptly, I turned and headed their way. Tyler and Ryan would understand, though I was sure they wouldn't. Every move I made these days seemed filled with drama.

I sat down next to Ben and across from Becca. She shoved a pile of construction paper my direction.

"We're making protest signs for the sit-in," she said.

"Yeah," Ben added, holding up his most recent creation. It read *Give Veg a Chance*. "Thought of it myself. You know, like *give love a chance*."

"Yeah, good for you," I grumbled back. Either he was forgetting our conversation from Saturday or intentionally rubbing it in. I could guess which. I picked up a marker and idly flipped it between my fingers.

Kirsten flashed a smile. "Becca called the newspaper. They're sending a photographer to cover the story!"

"And my father has a megaphone we can use," Becca announced. "I tried it at home. It's REALLY loud."

"Cool," Ben said, looking all too excited about the idea of using a megaphone at school. "I can tell jokes to get everyone's attention."

"About serving vegetarian entrées?" I asked.

Ben looked around the table. "Oh. Anyone know any vegetarian jokes?"

I could think of a joke all right. It involved a meat

float and a guy dressed up like a half rack of ribs. The thought made me shiver.

As if on cue, Becca changed the subject. "I hear the parade is really cool."

The marker slipped through my fingers.

"It's okay," Ben replied. "Most of the floats throw candy into the crowd. It's like Halloween, if you don't mind knocking a few toddlers out of the way."

"My church does a float every year," Jackson piped up. "My mom's in charge of it this year." He turned to Becca. "You can ride on it with me if you want."

"Oh, that sounds like fun," Becca replied. "I've never been on a float."

My jaw dropped next to the marker. I didn't know whether to punch Jackson or hug him. The thought of Becca riding on a float with that guy made me want to climb up on a step stool and yank out his chin hair. But if Becca was riding on a float, then odds were good she wouldn't see me riding on my dad's.

"Anyone else want to ride on the float?" Jackson asked.

Becca glanced at Kirsten. "I can't," Kirsten lamented. "My cousin is getting married that day and we have to leave early in the morning to go to her wedding."

Becca looked my way.

"Uh," I said, trying to think of a plausible excuse. "I promised to spend the day with my family." Hey, that was true.

"Oh, that's too bad," Jackson said with a genuine frown. "Our church does a float every year. You guys can ride on it next year."

"That sounds great," Kirsten said.

I picked up the marker and took a piece of construction paper. How could it be that the solution to my dilemma involved Becca spending the day with Jackson? And yet who was I to complain? If there was one thing I had discovered since meeting Becca, it was that lying was more stressful than you'd think. I was beginning to wonder if honesty might really be the best policy.

On the way to class, I caught up to Tyler and Ryan. "Hey, guys."

Ryan gave me a wave. "Hey, Stu."

Tyler gave me a different gesture. He still seemed miffed that I hadn't sat with them at lunch.

"Do you want to go to the carnival with us Friday night?" Ryan asked.

Judging from Tyler's demeanor, the answer I was about to give would not go over well. "I can't. I have plans already," I said, hoping my vagueness would be enough for them.

"Let me guess. You're going with your church group," Tyler said, his voice thick with sarcasm.

"No."

"Must be going with your family."

He knew that wasn't a reality. "Not quite."

"Then who?"

"Ben asked me to go with him."

"Just Ben?"

"And a couple others."

"Girls," Tyler said with distaste.

"Kirsten and Becca," I admitted.

"Instead of going with us," Tyler clarified for Ryan, "they're going with their girlfriends."

"They're not our girlfriends," I said with all the defense I could muster.

Tyler motioned for Ryan to follow as he turned and walked off toward class. "Have fun with your girlfriends."

Why was everyone so dramatic these days?

The remainder of the school week held more of the same. I continued to make sit-in signs at lunch with Becca and the other protestors. Tyler continued to ignore me. And I continued to stress over my double life as a vegetarian by day and meat eater at night. All in all, the week wasn't really so bad. If only it had ended before Friday night.

34

I spent Friday afternoon fretting over what to wear, what to do, and, in particular, what to say on a date. Not that this was technically a date, since neither Becca nor I had asked the other. But as far as I was concerned, it was my first date. Every possible scenario sprang to mind in which I could embarrass myself, including roller-coaster-induced vomiting, cotton-candy-induced vomiting, and vomiting brought on by other fits of vomiting. I wasn't paranoid—I was just afraid that everything and everyone was out to get my stomach.

My father popped by my room. "So I hear you're going to the carnival with Ben and a couple girls."

"Who told you that?"

"Mom."

Figured. "We're just friends."

My father eyed me like Harley had the weekend before. A smile curved his lips as he nodded with satisfaction. "You're a young man now. And a good one at that. Treat those girls nice. Show respect." He gave me a wink. "And if she wants a kiss, do you know what to do?"

That was the furthest thought from my mind. Up until that moment. Now it was the only thought in my mind. What would I do? I had watched TV. I understood what a kiss was. But suddenly all the mechanics involved seemed overwhelming. What do you do with your hands? Do your feet touch? Where do your arms go? Do you close your eyes? What *exactly* goes on with your lips?

My father nudged my shoulder. "Just enjoy the moment."

My mother called from downstairs. "Stu! Ben's here."

My father left my room with a parting nod. I sat staring at my shoes. After my father's comment, I wasn't ready to leave the house. I needed time to think.

But wasn't all my thinking what kept getting in the way? First, I was too slow choosing a square dancing partner. Then too slow in asking her to slow dance. And now I wanted a few months to understand the details of giving a proper kiss. So far, all my careful thinking had done me no good at all. I pulled on my shoes and grabbed a coat. For once, I would act without thinking. Just enjoy the moment. Yeah, right.

On the way to the carnival, Ben and I discussed how the date would work.

"The girls are meeting us at the entrance at seven. We can go on a few rides, get some snacks, and then head over to the games. Did you bring money?"

I pulled out a wad of bills. "This is all my allowance money since Christmas."

"How much you got there?"

"Twenty-seven dollars."

Ben stopped short. "Is that all? What sort of allowance is that?"

"I might have missed a few chores along the way."

"Dude."

"Shut up."

"You better hope Becca doesn't expect you to pay her way."

"Seriously? Do girls expect that?"

Ben shook his head. "Are you kidding? Have you watched movies? The guy always carries a lot of money, and the woman always spends it."

Ben's mother looked back at us. "What sort of movies have you been watching? This is the modern age. A woman does not go around spending her man's money. Unless he's foolish enough to let her," she added with a laugh. "You're too young to be paying a lady's way to anything. Just go have fun. And I'll be back to get you at nine thirty."

"I hope she's right," I whispered. Otherwise, I was going to need a real job. And I didn't like the sound of that.

The lights of the carnival lit up the night sky like a portable city. Smells of popcorn, cotton candy, corn dogs, and axle grease filled the air. Music blasted from speakers strung randomly about the grounds. All in all, it was about as awesome as a middle-school kid could hope for, short of a real-life zombie apocalypse.

In fact, if a zombie apocalypse were to occur, I couldn't think of a better place to enjoy the moment than in this wonderland of sights, smells, and shadowy places to hide. Ben and I got out of the car and headed for the main entrance.

"This is awesome!" Ben exclaimed.

"Yeah, almost better than *Death Intruders 4*," I replied, listening to the screams and occasional heaves of people on a ride called the Zipper. "If only there were rotting people chasing us."

Ben grinned. "That would be the best! Especially if there were chain saws lying around."

"And flamethrowers," I added. Zombies lacked the dexterity to work a flamethrower, which was a shame for them since there were so many lying about in *Death Intruders 4*. Lucky us.

We reached the front gate. Half an hour later, the girls still hadn't shown up.

"Do you think they're coming?" I asked.

"Yeah," Ben replied, "women are always late."

"How do you know that?"

Ben kicked at the ground. "My dad told me. He said women take forever getting ready and I better get used to waiting 'cause I'll be doing it for the rest of my life."

Really? I was usually the one my family had to wait for. "I liked it better when there weren't girls."

Ben giggled. "We'd be at the top of the Zipper barfing our guts out right now."

"Yeah, that'd be awesome."

Without warning, Kirsten and Becca materialized out of the darkness.

35

They approached looking—different. Both were wearing pink lipstick and mascara. Both had curled their hair. Both looked like they had stepped out of a teen magazine. The zombie warlord in my chest woke up and reminded me there were no chain saws, no flamethrowers, and no extra lives when it came to this type of apocalypse. If they had walked up and sucked the life right out of my chest, I would've died with my eyes bugging out and my lips frozen in a goofy grin.

"Hey, boys," Kirsten said.

"Hey, girls," Ben replied without missing a beat.

"Mbthmbth—" I mumbled like only I could.

"Hey, Stu," Becca said with a smile.

"Yes," I sputtered for no apparent reason.

"Let's go," Kirsten said. "I'm dying to ride the Zipper."

She led the way as we serpentined our way through the crowd. We found the entrance beneath a flashing sign that read *The Zipper—Zip at Your Own Risk*.

"Is that the ride?" Becca said, her eyes wide as she pointed at the cars dangling upside down above us.

"Yes," I replied. "Hardly anyone ever dies . . . that you hear about."

"How many die that you don't hear about?"

"Probably lots."

After a short wait, the ride operator ushered us to a car directly behind Ben and Kirsten. We climbed into a compartment that looked like the insides of a rusty barrel. The operator pulled our shoulder harnesses tight, then tested the buckles to make sure we were locked in.

"Is this ride safe?" Becca asked.

"Not particularly," he quipped, slamming the compartment door. "Enjoy the ride, little lady."

At this point, I felt like a photo I once saw of the first Russian cosmonaut. He was launched into orbit on the wafer-thin belief that a capsule the size of a hot tub could carry him into space and back again. All the while knowing that if the tiniest calculation proved incorrect, he'd disintegrate in a flash of cosmic glory.

Our car lurched upward while another car loaded. Ben and Kirsten waved at us through their rear window.

"Please keep your hands inside the cars at all times," came the voice of the ride operator over the PA system.

"Count down with us," Ben and Kirsten yelled.

Becca took my hand. "I'm scared."

Frankly, I was sweating a bit myself. "Hold on," I said.

"Five, four, three—" Ben and Kirsten shouted.

Our car bounced. Something that sounded like a transmission clanking into gear groaned below.

"Two, one, blastoff!" we yelled in unison with them.

An engine roared and our car swung upward like a catapult being released.

"AHH!!!" Becca screamed, squeezing my hand with the strength of a five-hundred-pound gorilla.

"AHH!!!" I screamed, hoping my hand wouldn't look like my nose before the ride was over.

"AAAAHHHHHH!!!!!!" we screamed together as the car reached the peak and flipped upside down.

"AAAAHHHHHH!!!!!" we screamed continuously as the ride alternated between rocketing us into space, then flinging us back at the ground. About halfway through, I concluded my mother making breakfast for dinner had been a bad idea.

"This is awesome!" Becca screamed in my ear.

"Yeah!" I screamed back, trying to keep down the pancakes and sausages I'd eaten.

At last, the ride slowed to a lurching stop and the operator freed us from our compartment of doom. We piled out, clinging to each other to keep from falling. Ben and Kirsten waited for us at the exit, giggling just like you'd expect.

"That was the best," Ben said as we stumbled together out the exit gate.

Kirsten grabbed Becca's arm. "Let's do it again!"

Becca shook her head. "No way. Once was enough for me. I thought I was gonna lose my dinner up there."

"Don't be a baby," I scolded, holding my stomach. "That was child's play."

"Then come with us!" Kirsten said, grabbing my arm.

I hadn't expected that. "That's okay. I'll stay here with Becca and look for a quiet place to die."

"Babies," Ben said with a laugh. "Although if I go again, I'll be joining you."

At that moment, we looked up to see a posse of middle schoolers approaching. It was mostly girls— and Jackson.

36

"Hi!" said Lisa, a girl I'd never noticed before but who appeared to have taken charge of the evening.

"Hi!" Kirsten and Becca said in unison.

After that, a lot of girl hugging took place. If boys hugged like that, a noogie brawl would break out. It would get ugly and probably mess up everyone's hair. When you get to my age, hair is one of the few things a guy can still control.

"We're on our way to the bumper cars!" Lisa said excitedly. Apparently anything said at the carnival had to be said excitedly.

Kirsten jumped up and down like a spastic cheerleader. "That sounds like fun!"

It's worth noting that the bumper cars at this carnival were more like bumper turtles. Old people with walkers could safely cross in front of them without risk of injury. The only time anyone got hurt was when they dozed off and hit their head on the padded steering wheel. However, from the reaction of the girls, this was going to be the most *AWESOME* ride *EVER*. It would probably eclipse square dancing and might even contend with their last birthday sleepover.

Jackson nodded from the far side of the girl crowd. He would have come over to say hello, but a gaggle of girls were holding his arms like he was some sort of Thanksgiving Day parade balloon. Poor guy. He just couldn't catch a break.

Surprisingly, there was no line at the bumper cars when we arrived. Apparently, the toddler crowd had moved on to Miss Myrtle's Magical Merry-Go-Round and left this bad boy to us. By tucking my knees up to my chest, I was able to squeeze into my car. How Jackson fit into his I don't know. From the looks of it, he'd need a can opener to get out. Ben gave me a thumbs-up from his car, which told me just how much he was into Kirsten. The last time anyone forced him to go on the bumper cars, he gave them a noogie that left a permanent dent in their head. You can still see it behind my left ear. We were five at the time.

The operator gave us a few instructions that amounted to "please don't get up and leave before the ride is over no matter how lame it is." With that, he turned on the electricity and the cars lurched forward an inch at a time. I found myself sufficiently bored right up until I caught a flash of motion from behind. The next thing I knew, my car was pushed up against the railing. I turned to find Jackson heading away. He wove in and out of traffic as if the cars were standing still, which some were. And then he bumped into Becca's car just hard enough to make her giggle.

I'd seen enough. I turned and gave chase. What I mean is I turned and lurched my way forward like an angry snail. In the meantime, Jackson circled the oval course again, and slammed me into the center barrier. Some guys have all the luck. He got the one bumper car that could actually move. I eased my car away from the barrier, then made the bold decision to drive in the opposite direction. The operator shouted a stern warning, something to the effect of I would be forced to go on the ride a second time if I didn't follow the rules. Undeterred, I bore down on Jackson as he came 'round again.

They say revenge is best served cold. That seemed odd since all I felt was hot and cramped in my turtle-mobile. Perhaps that's why I didn't see Gretchen bearing down on me from the side. To make a slow story short, Jackson zipped past just before Gretchen nuzzled me into the far corner. Both cars refused to budge. Agonizing minutes went by as we both worked to free our useless pile-of-crud cars. At last, the operator put us both out of our misery by turning the electricity off and ending the ride.

"Hope you had as much fun as I did," he said with a yawn.

On the fun scale, it had been right behind getting stitches and having my nose reset. Strangely, everyone else seemed to have had a grand time.

"That was AMAZING!" Lisa said loudly enough to make the ride operator drop his cigarette.

"We should do it again!" Kirsten agreed.

"I don't know, it was kind of scary," said a girl who wasn't joking.

Jackson ambled off toward the game area. A half dozen girls followed. That seemed to sway the rest of the group as we followed the plinking and plunking sounds of air rifles being fired, Ping-Pong balls clinking off glass plates, and money being changed at an alarming rate. Giant stuffed animals lured us in promising fame and fortune to anyone lucky enough to win. The girls oohed and aahed over the prizes, stating their choices just loudly enough for any hero-in-the-making to hear.

I, for one, was trying to figure out what had happened to the "date" I was supposed to be on. Becca appeared on the far side of the group, inches closer to Jackson than me. It was enough to make my stomach churn.

Try as I might, I couldn't navigate through the sea of girls, concession stands, and rigged games to reach her. In a moment of weakness, I was lured over to a stand selling corn dogs. If there's one thing that every carnival needs, it's a corn dog stand. Pairing corn bread with hot dogs had been a moment of culinary brilliance. Deep-frying the concoction took it to the level of genius worthy of song. I plunked my hard-earned allowance down and took possession of a golden-brown piece of perfection jammed on a stick. All it needed was a little ketchup and mustard to send me to corn dog paradise.

"What's that?"

Oh, ship. I turned to find Becca beside me.

"This?" I said, pointing at the only thing in my hand. "This? This is for Ben." I hung my head as I handed my beautiful golden taste treat to my best friend. "Here. Eat it and die."

"Thanks," Ben said, stuffing the corn dog, stick and all, into his mouth. Geez, he has a big mouth. He slid the naked stick out and handed it back. I hate that guy.

37

A commotion brought our attention to where Jackson stood before a game so insidious I had refused to go near it in the past. Actually, I had spent hours watching men of all shapes and sizes try their luck to no avail. The challenge seemed simple enough. A rope ladder had been stretched at a forty-five-degree angle between two hooks. The object was to climb the ladder and ring the bell at the top. This seemed simple enough, until you realized the two hooks were free spinning, meaning the slightest imbalance would flip the ladder upside down, throwing the climber off onto a mat below. Seeing a crowd forming, the operator climbed up the ladder and rang the bell with the dexterity of a circus acrobat.

"Anyone man enough?" he said, eyeing all the men present. Since there were no men present, his eyes came to rest on Jackson, Ben, and me.

The legion of giggling girls around Jackson pushed him forward. He responded by flexing for the crowd, which brought an audible "ooh." He then climbed up on stage and grabbed hold of the ladder. Keeping his body low like a stalking panther, he shinnied his way up the ladder without missing a beat and rang the bell.

From the screaming that ensued, you would have thought he had just saved the universe. This, of course, led to another round of flexing for the crowd. I didn't have enough testosterone in my body to throw up a manly goose bump, let alone a muscle that could be seen through skintight cotton.

Kirsten pushed Ben forward. "Your turn."

This brought on another round of screaming from the increasingly raucous group of girls. Seriously, they needed a boy band to stop by so they could get their groupie-ness out before someone got hurt, or lost their hearing. In the meantime, Ben walked forward and faced the ladder. Throwing a confident grin at his fan base, he mounted the ropey beast. The operator lifted his microphone and fueled the crowd into a further frenzy.

"Ladies and gentlemen, we just had our first winner all evening. Is it possible we'll have two in a row?"

I could see Ben trembling as he tried to keep the ladder steady, the veins in his neck bulging from the effort. He moved his feet one rung up, bringing his hands and feet almost together. His back bowed like a cornered cat. The ladder shook as he coiled himself. How it didn't flip over was a Christmas miracle. And then he did something only Ben could be stupid enough to attempt. He leapt like a bullfrog. Doing so without flipping the ladder deserved a footnote in the *Guinness World Records* under the category Acts That Can Only Be Done Under the Influence of Adrenaline. Everyone gasped. With one flailing hand, Ben smacked the ringer on the bell before crashing to the mat below in a heap of glory.

The response from the crowd was deafening. The ground shook like an earthquake. Windows in nearby towns probably shattered. I couldn't help but give him a single clap, I was that moved. Ben stood and bowed to the crowd, basking in the moment. The game operator shook his hand as he gave him a stuffed animal the size of a whale, which incidentally *was* a whale. Ben immediately gave it to Kirsten to a round of "aww" from the crowd. My eyes watered. With envy. Being a true friend, Ben quieted the crowd, then pointed in my direction.

"You're up!" he called out.

At this point, Ben could have called an infant up and the crowd would have gone wild. And given recent events, the baby probably would have taken its first steps crossing the ladder before doing a backflip to ring the bell. However, I was no baby, no matter how badly I wanted to be at that moment. Unfortunately, I was forced to march like a man up onto the stage to the chant of "STU, STU, STU!"

"For the first time in the history of this great carnival," the operator shouted into the microphone, "two young men in a row have rung the bell!" He turned to me. "Tell me, will you be the third?"

38

The response from the crowd made it clear they believed, even if I had to grow wings and fly my way to the bell. I would have given anything for a genie that could grant that kind of wish. No such luck. Not even the psychic from the palm reading tent made an appearance. That left two choices: run away screaming or run away crying *and* screaming. It was a difficult choice.

I took hold of the ladder. The ropes felt firm, almost inviting. The ladder was really quite short, not more than ten feet in length. I could see now how Ben had been able to leap his way to the end. The operator stepped close.

"Move like a lizard lifting opposing arms and legs. And don't fall," he said with a small maniacal laugh.

The art of the small maniacal laugh is underrated. Let me tell you, it's a highly effective way to scare the bejeezus out of a young man facing a medieval test of manhood. Take me for example. It was all I could do to take hold of the rope while squeezing my bladder shut at the same time. At any moment, I risked losing one or the other, and I could only hope it'd be the rope.

I eased myself up until my body was off the ground. The ladder felt stable so long as I lay perfectly still. Behind me, the crowd began to murmur. I slid my left hand and right foot up a rung. I let out a sigh of relief. The first rung hadn't been so bad. That's when I felt a tiny shudder run through the ropes.

"You're on your own now," the operator whispered.

He'd been holding it steady? The thought hit me like a load of bricks. Apparently literally, because the ladder shook violently, then flipped before I could plead for mercy. I clung on for dear life. That is, my hands clung. My feet had never clung to anything in their life and weren't about to now. I hung for a moment like the butt end of a bad joke. Were I an acrobat, or a gymnast, or a little girl, I would have deftly swung my feet up and climbed back on. However, I was none of those. In the time it took the crowd to gasp, my fingers slipped and I tumbled onto the mat like a crumpled leaf.

"Oh, that's too bad," the operator shouted to the crowd. "So close. Who's next?"

I crawled off the mat. I would have continued crawling if it were not for Ben's legs blocking my path. "Dude, that was hilarious!"

"Shut up."

He gave me a hand off the ground. "No, seriously. It was awesome!"

"Where's your whale? I'd like to shove it up your—"

"C'mon, you have to admit that was pretty crazy."

I shook myself off. "The only crazy thing is that I agreed to get up there."

"You're a rock star."

If any part of my body had been a rock, I would have crushed Ben's head with it. As it was, all I could do was smile and hope he'd get food poisoning from my corn dog.

Kirsten and Becca were waiting near the coin toss booth.

"That looked scary," Becca said with admiration in her voice.

"Not really," I replied. "More like terrifying."

That brought a giggle. From Ben.

Meanwhile, Kirsten was showing off her life-sized whale to Gretchen.

"Can you believe it?" she said.

"That was so cool," Gretchen said, eyeing Ben while completely ignoring me. She held up a stuffed dolphin that looked more like a stuffed gym sock. "Isn't it cute?"

I'd seen cuter in my laundry basket.

Gretchen pointed to a boy hidden on the other side of the booth. "He won it at one of the shooting games and gave it to me."

The boy came over. My jaw dropped. Ryan stood next to Gretchen. He saw us and smiled, the blush on his face matching hers perfectly.

Before I had time to adjust to the shock of Ryan and Gretchen together, Tyler showed up. With a girl. And not just any girl. He walked up with Annie, the girl in our school most likely to be chosen for the cover of a teen magazine. And she was smiling at him. At

Tyler? Our Tyler? True, he was kinda tall. And had perfectly coiffed hair. And fine features including sleek, supple lips.

Honestly, who was I kidding? I had no idea what he looked like. I couldn't recognize a good-looking guy if one dropped on me with a sign that read *Hey, stupid. I'm good-looking.* When I checked out a guy, I mostly saw *dork* written across their forehead, especially if they had made the mistake of going to sleep early at one of Ben's sleepovers.

Tyler walked over with a grin that was all too familiar. I'd seen it on Ben, and in the mirror. He was wearing the smitten look that he'd carry until either she dumped him or he woke up.

"Hey, guys," Tyler said.

"What's up?" Ben asked.

"Not much. Just hangin' at the carnival."

Ben looked at Annie. "Yes, I see that."

"I thought you didn't like girls," I added.

"Shut up."

Poor chap. He had no idea the world he'd walked into.

He leaned in. "Hey, have you ever kissed a girl?"

That brought the zombie warlord to life. I'd almost forgotten my earlier conversation with my father. Ben and I both shook our heads.

"Well, I have. Tonight," he finished.

Ben and I gaped.

"Son of a ditch digger," Ben answered for both of us. "Where?"

"Behind the palm reader's booth. It just kinda happened."

My hands were sweating. So were my armpits. In fact, my whole body had begun to sweat. Off to the side, I saw Annie, Kirsten, and Becca giggling. That didn't look good. Were they having the same conversation? Becca caught my eye. She smiled, then looked away. The zombie warlord banged on my chest for all he was worth. "What time is it?"

Tyler checked his watch. "Nine forty."

Ben grunted. "Seriously? Dang it, my mom's probably waiting for us."

"That's too bad," I chimed in. "Guess we gotta go."

"Next year I'm driving myself," Ben muttered.

"In what? A go-cart?"

"Anything would be better than coming with my mom."

He had a point. We gave Tyler a high five, then stopped by the girls.

"See ya, we gotta go," Ben said.

"Really?" Kirsten asked with pouty lips. "It's early."

"I know. My mom is a pain."

"I gotta go, too," Becca said.

She joined us as we headed out front.

"This was really fun," she said.

"Super fun," Ben agreed.

"Awesome," I half-heartedly threw in.

We found Becca's mom waiting at the entrance. Becca gave a final wave as they drove off.

When I got home, my father was waiting for me. "So, did anyone get lucky with a kiss tonight?" he asked with a sly grin.

Yes, as a matter of fact, someone had gotten lucky. But not me. "Nope."

He frowned. "Oh, well. Maybe next time."

I headed up to bed. Yeah, right.

39

I woke Saturday to blue skies and a knot the size of a half rack of ribs in my stomach. The reality hit me that Becca would be riding on a float with Jackson. The two of them would spend the day being chummy while I'd be riding on a float with my little brother and a bunch of guys dressed up like sides of beef. To make matters worse, my other friends would see me. Any one of them could give me away Monday to Becca. How had I not thought of that before? I needed a way out. And quick.

Before I even got the covers off, my father charged in, a wild look in his eye.

"Get up!" he shouted like a crazy man about to do something crazy with the help of other crazies. "I told you to be ready." He jammed a piece of dry toast into my mouth and threw back the covers. "Let's go. Don't break your promise to me now."

For starters, I had made no promises. Nor had I been given any sort of morning timeline. The parade didn't start until noon. "What are you talking about?" I grumbled, sitting up.

The wild look on my father's face only got wilder. "The parade is today! Have you forgotten? We have to be in line by ten thirty! What are you doing?"

The clock showed 8:30 a.m. But, more important, I had lost my chance to prepare a convincing sickness that would get me out of going. With toast jammed in my mouth and my clothes being thrown at me from all angles, it was too late to improvise. I pulled on a shirt and pants as my father dragged me out the door.

We rushed out to his truck, which refused to start. "What the—" he shouted at the key, as if it were taking part in a conspiracy. He twisted the key in the ignition, but still nothing happened. He pounded the dashboard in frustration then let loose with a string of expletives that would have melted the ignition of a lesser vehicle.

"Where's Tommy?" I asked to pass the time. When my father went on a rant, it could last awhile.

My father finally inserted the key all the way, which did a lot to explain why the truck hadn't started sooner. The engine roared to life, and we shot out of the driveway. "He's . . . with your mother."

"Oh. Where's Mom?"

My father careened out of our cul-de-sac and barreled through a four-way stop. "I took her to Harley's barn last night and surprised her with the float," he said grimly.

I tried to imagine her face. A shudder ran through me. "Why did you do that?"

We slid around a sharp corner. "She wouldn't allow Tommy to be in the parade unless I showed her what we were doing."

"Is he going to be in the parade?"

"No. They're out running . . . errands."

"What about me?"

He sped through a red light with a casual shrug. "She said you were old enough to decide for yourself if you wanted to take part in such foolishness."

From past experience, my mother had a pretty good

understanding of foolishness. "I'm not sure I do want to take part."

My father slid sideways into Harley's driveway. "Sure you do. It's going to be fun," he said as we skidded to a stop in front of Harley's barn. The barn doors were already open. The float sat in the semidarkness like a mythical beast waiting to pounce on unwary travelers. Harley ran from the back door of his house dressed in his full ham hock outfit, complete with bone-in cap that jutted off his head like a giant infected pimple.

"It's about time you got here. The other boys are in the house having a little breakfast."

As if on cue, the rest of the crew streamed out to greet us. Before me stood everything from a whole roasted chicken to a three-hundred-pound lamb chop. Incidentally, Joe, the guy wearing the lamb chop outfit, really did weigh three hundred pounds. Today he looked closer to four hundred. I wondered if that had been taken into account when purchasing the trailer.

"Men," my father said, stepping up onto the running board of his truck like a platform, "for far too long we've stood by while others"—he said *others* with added contempt—"have touted the virtues of eating less meat." He paused for effect.

Harley encouraged him to continue. "Hurry up, we're already late."

My father raised his hands to placate the crowd. "Today, we take a stand. Today, we go where no meat lover has gone before." He clenched his fists and raised them to the heavens. "Today, we go down in infamy!"

I was pretty sure my father was using the word *infamy* incorrectly. Last I checked, it worked for describing a sneak attack on Pearl Harbor but not so much when describing a parade float.

A round of laughter came from all around. "Hear, hear!" his comrades shouted. "Whatever you say, boss."

I followed the group into the barn for a last loving look at their creation before we headed out. A sign had been added to the front bumper that read *Truly Meats, Since 1964*. Signs had also been hung on either side of the trailer with big, bold letters that, unfortunately, were clear enough to be read. One said *Stop by for a Meat & Greet*. The other said *Be Truly to Yourself—Eat*

Meat. Along the top of the float, papier-mâché animals had been attached with cuts of meat outlined on their torsos. I took a deep breath. It was going to be a long afternoon.

My father eased his truck into the barn. Any hope of a mishap went unfulfilled as the trailer clunked onto the hitch. The gang loaded into the back of the truck, leaving me to ride shotgun.

"Better get your costume on," my father said to me. "We'll be to town in no time."

I stared at the pile of stockings next to me. With a small sigh, I pulled off my clothes and pulled on the suit.

"Lookin' good," my father said.

What I looked like was a stocking leg with a compound fracture. "Yeah, thanks."

The meat float got more than a few stares as we drove into town. At last, we pulled onto a side street near the beginning of the parade route and took our place behind a line of other waiting floats. When I say *floats*, I mean beautifully crafted creations full of fresh flowers, bright colors, and cheery goodwill, including the one in front of us carrying the Irrigation Festival royalty. Riding atop sat the queen and her court, a lovely group of young ladies in long, flowing dresses with elbow-length white gloves already smiling, despite the ungodly early hour.

I quickly checked the other floats in line ahead of us. None contained Jackson's church group. I let out a sigh of relief.

The guys piled out of the back of the truck. The queen turned. Her mouth dropped. She opened it as if to scream. But nothing came out. Her fellow princesses saw the shocked look on her face and followed her stare. "What is that?" I heard one whisper. "I don't know, but I'm not riding in front of *that*," another replied.

My father pulled on his bratwurst costume. This probably didn't help matters. "Hello, ladies," he said in greeting.

That didn't seem to get the response he was expecting. One of the princesses hopped down and went over to a man dressed in a chauffer suit. She pointed in our direction while giving him an earful of instruction. The driver nodded, climbed into his compartment, started the engine, and drove the float up over the sidewalk and down an alley out of sight.

"That was rude," Harley said, standing next to my father.

My father shook his head. "I'm sure it wasn't us."

I'm sure it was. I began to wonder if we'd be the first float ever to be banned from the parade before the parade even started. The idea sounded pretty reasonable. A man with an official badge walked over to my father. He gave us a puzzled once-over, then handed my father an entry number.

"You'll be in about the middle, just behind the Can-Can Youth Drill Team and just before the Port Townsend High School marching band." He gave us a last quizzical look and hurried away.

My father turned to his crew, holding up our float number. "Well, boys, it's official. We're in the parade."

This brought on a lot more cheering than seemed appropriate, given that our town's royalty had just snuck down an alley to get away from us. After that, not much happened for a really long time, pretty much forever. Being in a parade was not nearly as exciting as

I expected. Mostly, you sat around waiting your turn and grumbling about how long could it take for a bunch of motorized flowerpots to get moving.

In the distance came the sounds of drums banging, gospel choirs singing, and the crack of muskets being fired. A parade is not a parade without men dressed up like Davy Crockett randomly firing muskets. Which would be handy if a zombie apocalypse were to break out. But otherwise gets pretty annoying.

From the comments being made, the guys on our float were getting hungry, and I began to wonder if they understood our costumes weren't real food.

"Is that BBQ sauce you're cooked in?" Joe asked, staring at my ribs.

"Uh, I don't know. I think it's just a brown marker."

He let out a sigh. "Too bad. I prefer BBQ sauce."

Yikes. It was time to get this party started.

40

Just before an act of cannibalism occurred, we finally got the nod from the parade official to move forward. My father hopped in the truck, which wasn't easy dressed as a giant bratwurst. The rest of us took up positions on the float, not coordinated positions, mind you. We milled about like meat-entrée pirates drifting out to sea on a derelict ship. The float crawled forward at a speed slightly slower than the bumper car I had driven the night before.

Just before we turned onto Main Street, my mother appeared with my little brother. He was dressed in his chicken leg costume, complete with bone sticking out his backside and everything. They approached my father.

"This really is the dumbest thing ever," my mom said to my dad.

My father gave her a kiss out the window. "I know. I'm beginning to think you might be right."

"Beginning to think?" my mother asked. She looked the float over from beginning to end. A smile creased her lips. "I hate to say it, but there is an odd sort of small-town charm to the thing. And a real sense of history."

"Really?" my father asked.

"Truly," she replied with a genuine grin.

My father let out a whoop. "The party's on," he called back to us. "Let's have some fun with this thing, shall we?"

My mother walked back to the trailer and helped Tommy up.

"That's the best-looking drumstick ever," Joe said, giving Tommy a high five.

"Yes, let's keep him that way," my mother replied.

"Don't you worry," Harley said, lifting Tommy up onto his shoulders. "We'll take good care of this little guy."

My mother turned to me. "Need anything?"

Yes, a way out. "I'm okay."

"Okay?" Joe exclaimed. "Look at him. He's a star."

A star that comes served with a side of corn and mashed potatoes. "Yeah. A star."

My mother smiled. "Have fun. By the way, I'm making ribs for dinner," she said with a wink as she turned to go. "It seemed fitting."

With that, we turned onto Main Street. Both sides of the street were lined with people, more people than I had seen in one place before. They were clapping and waving at the drill team in front of us, which had stopped to twirl about, stomping their boots in unison like a herd of tap-dancing buffalo. Harley dropped Tommy down beside me.

"It's showtime," Joe said, puffing up.

The last thing Joe needed was to puff up anymore. If he got any larger, we'd need a second float for the rest of us.

My father inched his way forward until we reached the first onlookers. All eyes turned to us. My heart started to hammer. We were now hemmed in by people on both sides. Their faces held a mixture of shock, confusion, and laughter.

"Pick yourself up one of these lamb chops," Joe called out, thumping his chest.

That brought a roar of laughter from the crowd.

Joe lumbered across the float. "Me—it's what's for dinner," he called out to the onlookers on the other side of the street.

Another roar of laughter.

Joe did his best strongman pose. We all joined in. Tommy got the biggest response when he flexed his little arms for the crowd.

"Look at the mighty drumstick," someone in the crowd shouted.

Harley lifted Tommy up for all to see.

"I'm a mighty drumstick," Tommy shouted back.

The crowd went wild. Camera phones appeared from all angles. People ran into the street to be photographed next to our float.

"Time for the piñatas," Joe shouted to us. He pulled a baseball bat from its hiding place. "Stand back," he warned us.

He climbed up some steps to where the papier-mâché animals hung, then reared back with the bat like a home-run hitter. I pulled Tommy close as Joe swung with full force. A bunny rabbit exploded into a cloudburst of red licorice that sprayed over the crowd. Some shrieked. Others ran. No one dared touch the candy that lay splattered around them.

Action was needed. Quickly. "Harley, how about you let me and Tommy give out the candy?" I pleaded with my best non-pleading tone.

Harley looked out at the stunned faces of the children, some with bits of red licorice stuck in their hair. He took the bat from Joe. "Yeah, maybe that would be a good idea."

I pulled the remaining piñatas down and went to work prying them open. Tommy helped by getting his sobs under control. "Why did he kill the bunny?" he kept asking.

There really was no answer to that question, so I ignored it by giving him a chocolate bar from the intestinal tract of the piglet I'd just opened. I hopped down and approached the nearest group of kids.

Holding out the surgically opened piglet, I let them reach inside for a treat. "That's gross," one of them said. "Can I have another?"

Before long, the piglet's insides were empty. Tommy brought over a brightly colored rooster. Together, we passed out the candy corn inside. Everyone wanted photos with us. Pretty soon all the guys had hopped off the float to mingle with the crowd. We slowly made our way along the parade float basking in the glory of being a surprise sensation. My mouth actually got tired from smiling. Even old-timers wanted a photo with me and Tommy. "Your grampa used to come in on Sunday morning just so I could have the pick of the lamb for dinner after church," one elderly woman said, clasping my hand. "He was a fine man."

My father waved to the crowd. He honked every time he saw someone he knew. The honking was continuous. Until that moment, I never realized how many people knew my father. Apparently, if you want to be popular, own a butcher shop.

By the time we reached the hardware store where Ben's father worked, I was having the time of my life.

"HEY, STU!" Ben yelled.

I looked up to see him and a mob of others sitting on the roof of the hardware store. Clearly, they had the best seats in the house. I waved, trying my best to look studly.

"GET A LOOK AT THESE RIBS," I shouted.

"COME TO MY HOUSE FOR DINNER," Ben shouted. "YOU'RE MAKING ME HUNGRY."

I flexed. "YOU CAN'T HANDLE THESE RIBS."

I tossed the last of the candy up to them. This brought a round of hollering from the group, except one girl I noticed standing apart. One girl staring down at me with a look of shock and terror. One girl who glanced away the moment our eyes met. Becca. It couldn't be. The zombie warlord in my chest hammered to be let out. What was she doing up there? She was supposed to be riding on a float with Jackson. That's when I noticed Jackson standing next to her.

The float pulled forward around the parade's final corner.

I was doomed.

41

Sunday is meant to be a day of rest. But not that Sunday. I spent the morning in a state of complete worry. Worry that left fingernail marks in both palms from squeezing my fists as I paced back and forth in my room. By noon, I had reached one simple conclusion: I was an idiot. Only an idiot could have believed he'd survive the parade with his meat-eating secret intact. A merely dim-witted guy would have seen through that wishful thinking in an instant. A somewhat intelligent young man would never have gotten into this predicament in the first place. There was no denying it. I was an idiot. No, not just an idiot. I was a blubbering, completely stupid, total loser of an idiot. There's a difference. And it's not subtle.

By afternoon, I couldn't stand the sight, or smell, of my room. I ran to Ben's house. I didn't run for the exercise but to avoid being seen by Becca.

Ben pulled me into his room. "Dude, you are SO screwed."

That was not the encouragement I came looking for. "Shut up."

Ben sprawled across his bed. "Classic, man. Classic. You convince her you're a vegetarian and then show up dressed like a rack of ribs. You should have seen the look on your face when you realized she was standing there."

I tried to suffocate Ben with his pillow, but it only covered half his face. "Why didn't you tell me she was with you?"

Ben slid his head out from under the pillow and sat up. "Dude, you don't have a cell phone."

There's nothing worse than being told the obvious.

"Besides," he continued, "she and Jackson showed up right before you got there. Their float finished early, so they came back to watch the rest of the parade with us."

I flopped onto my back. "I'm such an idiot. How did things get so out of control?"

"Well, you did lie to her about being a vegetarian."

"Shut up."

"And wore a meat costume in front of the whole town."

"Shut up."

"And then flexed your meaty ribs right in front of her."

"I said *shut up*!"

"I guess things just happen."

Ben is the worst giggler ever.

"What am I supposed to do now?"

The giggles stopped. "I don't know, dude. Really, I don't know."

Yeah, neither did I.

42

Monday morning arrived like a punch in the gut. Not the sort of punch your friend gives you after you accidentally chain-saw him in half playing *Death Intruders*. This was the sort of punch that makes you wish you had a 105-degree fever to keep you home until the end of the school year.

"Ninety-eight point six," my mother said, pulling the thermometer out of my mouth.

No such luck. "Maybe I should stay home today as a precautionary measure."

My mother furrowed her brows. "Stu, do you have a test today that you didn't study for?"

Why would she jump to that conclusion? "No."

"Big assignment due?"

"No."

"Square dancing is over—it can't be that."

That's for darn sure.

She studied my face. "What's going on?"

What's going on? Becca saw me wearing a rack of ribs costume. She knows I'm a liar. My life is ruined. That's what's going on. "Nothing."

Her eyes held mine. I could feel them boring into my skull searching for secrets.

I threw the covers back. "All right, I'm getting up. Just give me a minute."

She stood and walked to the door. "Thank goodness. You were starting to scare me."

After she left, I considered my options. I could sit with Becca at lunch and pretend nothing had changed. Or I could admit that everything had changed and spend lunch alone in the boys' room. The first option needed her to be okay with us pretending everything was okay. Judging by the look on her face Saturday that seemed unlikely. That left the second option. I sighed and headed downstairs for breakfast. It would have to keep me going until dinner.

The ride to school gave me plenty of time to work up a stomach full of butterflies. I had no idea so many butterflies could fit in one stomach. By the time I got out of the car, the fluttering made it hard to walk. Or maybe it was the fact that Ben was pulling on my backpack.

"Dude. What are you going to tell her?"

"I'm not going to tell her anything. I'm just going to hide and hope she doesn't notice me. Got a better plan?"

Ben laughed, but his face looked pinched. "Dude, we're meeting at lunch to work on signs for the sit-in."

The butterflies swirled into a tornado in my stomach. "Yeah, about that—"

Ben clapped me on the shoulder. "You better think of something quick."

My cheeks felt hot. Why couldn't my mom take my temperature now? I'd be back home in bed for sure. "Yeah, thanks."

The bell rang. He pulled me toward class. "C'mon, it's just a girl. Right?"

Yeah, right.

At lunchtime, I slunk to the back of the cafeteria and sat alone with my hood up and my head down. It seemed better than spending lunch hiding in a bathroom stall. At least I could breathe without gagging. My ham sandwich tasted like sawdust. So did my apple and my candy bar. Even my chocolate milk made my mouth dry. I closed my lunch bag.

"Dude, what are you doing?" Ben asked, helping himself to the rest of my candy bar.

"What do you think I'm doing? I'm praying the world ends so I don't have to face her."

"That may be difficult."

"Why?"

Ben moved out of the way. Behind him stood Becca. She placed a pin on the table next to my lunch sack.

"This is yours," she said before walking away.

The message on the pin read *Vegetarians Unite!* I looked around to see that everyone taking part in the sit-in was wearing one, even Ben.

"Dude—" Ben started.

"Shut up."

"I'm just saying—"

"Shut up."

Ben returned to his table. I kept my head bowed, searching the floor for a hole to crawl into. Not a hole anywhere.

43

That night at dinner my father was all grins.

"You will not believe the day I've had," he said between mouthfuls of stew. "The shop was hopping all day. At one point we had a line of customers out the door. I've never seen anything like it."

"That's wonderful," my mother said.

"I don't like stew," my brother added, clearly focused on his own agenda.

"I don't like you, either," I threw in just in case he meant *Stu*, not *stew*.

My mother turned on both of us. "Don't be rude. Your father has had a good day."

"Yay, Dad," I mumbled to my bowl. I should have been happy for him. But I was stuck like my little brother on my own agenda. I envied the kid. His biggest issue in life was meat being served in broth. For me, my whole life was an issue.

After dinner, I sat in my room staring at the homework on my desk that wasn't going to get done. Finally, I pulled the pin from my backpack. *Vegetarians Unite!* I was neither vegetarian nor united with her cause. The pin went back into my backpack to keep me from using it to poke my own eyes out. Why had I lied to her? Maybe I had just been naive. No, not even I could buy that load of chipotle. Idiot remained the only answer.

The next day at school, I continued my lunchroom exile. It seemed the only option short of moving away and changing my identity. Maybe when I was older and could drive, but for now I was better off living at home no matter how attractive the name Armando seemed.

My exile would have been easier if the sounds of giggling didn't keep coming my way.

"C'mon, dude," Ben said, giggling in my ear. "It's not that bad. She hasn't even looked your way."

That did not help my mood. "Thanks, I feel so much better."

"You're making too big a deal of this."

I set my turkey sandwich down. "Too big a deal? She thought I was a vegetarian. My dad owns a butcher shop. I can barely stand the sight of vegetables, let alone eat them." My shoulders slumped. "I'm such an idiot."

Ben took a seat. "I admit you screwed up big-time. Even worse than that time you tried to bleach your own hair."

My scalp winced.

"But, dude, you can't just hide over here forever."

Why not? It wasn't like Ben to get all reasonable on me. Or to even have a point. That had never been his strong suit. Although I had to admit my current plan did seem a bit shortsighted. "Maybe tomorrow," I threw out to get him off my back.

"All righty, then." He stood to go. "Tomorrow."

Tomorrow came and went with me convincing Tyler and Ryan to forgo their sudden interest in sitting with girls at lunch. The three of us hunkered down at my new table in the far corner of the lunchroom.

"What are we doing here?" Ryan asked.

I rolled my eyes as if he had just asked the

dumbest thing ever. "We're being ourselves. No girls. Just us guys."

"We're helping him hide from Becca," Tyler added. "Until he can man up and deal with what he did."

Nothing could be further from the truth. "Shut up."

The three of us sullenly ate together. With the topic of girls being off the table, there didn't seem much else to talk about.

Thursday was just about as lame. Tyler made an excuse to leave us for a minute. He went and sat with Ben and the others and didn't come back.

"That was a cheap trick," I remarked.

"Wish I had thought of it first," Ryan said, glancing over to where Gretchen sat.

"We don't need 'em."

Ryan set his sandwich down. "I'm not sitting in the corner all alone for the rest of the year just because you're afraid of her."

That may have been the boldest thing Ryan had ever said. His words struck me like a zombie slap in the face.

"What am I supposed to do? She hates me."

"You don't know that. You don't know anything."

Knowing Ryan, I was pretty sure that made two of us. "You should have seen her face."

He turned toward me. "You should see yours."

Pretty sure he wasn't talking about my nose. "The whole thing sucks."

Ryan nodded. "Yeah. Sucks."

44

In PE, Mr. Snedaker had us sit on the gym bleachers. "Let's see how your diet has changed since the first time we reviewed your notebooks."

I opened mine to the most recent page. My breath caught in my throat. Green beans? I had eaten green beans? And tomato? And raw carrots? And WHOLE WHEAT bread? Wait, that's right. I had just eaten whole wheat bread at lunch. The shock of it hit me. I LIKED whole wheat bread. When had that happened? I leafed backward through my notebook. The names of other vegetables stared up at me beginning with Joe's Smokin' Peas.

"Mr. Truly," I heard Mr. Snedaker say. "Any changes since you began tracking what you eat?"

I nodded, unable to find the words to break the news.

Ben peered over my shoulder. "This week he's eaten green beans and tomato and—what the—?"

"That's right," I said proudly. "I tried a piece of kale."

Murmurs passed through the crowd. Murmurs of indifference, mind you. No one else really seemed to care. Except I did notice a pair of eyes turned in my direction a few rows over.

"Well done, Mr. Truly," commended Mr. Snedaker. "Sounds like some real progress has happened in your food life. What brought about your curiosity in new foods?"

"Well, sir," I began. "I, uh, realized there are people who actually like vegetables." My eyes flicked to Becca and back, not daring to hang there long enough to catch her reaction. "And—I thought, well—maybe I should give 'em more of a chance."

The boys behind me snickered. I chose to ignore them.

"I didn't even realize until just now when I checked

my journal. I guess sometimes things change and you don't even know it."

"Yes, that has absolutely been my hope," Mr. Snedaker responded, his hands raising to heaven. "There are so many interesting foods, and so many of them are good for you."

I glanced back down at my journal, still not believing what was written there. And it was the truth. For the first time in weeks, I felt free of the burden of making up lies to cover up my real self. Maybe I really was changing for the better. I looked up to find Becca's eyes on mine. She gave me a look that seemed pleased and hurt all at the same time. Then she glanced away.

I spent the afternoon in my room thinking about everything that had happened recently. First, Becca had shown up. And then my brain had gone all crazy. And now my journal had revealed a shocking interest in vegetables that I never knew existed until I met Becca. It was crazy, as crazy as inviting zombies over for dinner. BTW, don't do that. Ben and I learned that the hard way in level sixteen of *Death Intruders 3*.

Someone knocked on my bedroom door.

"Yeah," I grumbled in my best, you-don't-want-to-come-in-here voice.

My father opened the door. "Everything okay? You haven't seemed quite yourself this week."

Hadn't I? What would've given that impression? "I'm good."

Apparently my tone wasn't convincing. My father closed the door behind him and took a seat on my bed. "I'm not the most sensitive guy, but something's going on here. Girl trouble?"

Why did everyone keep jumping to that conclusion? "Maybe."

"Do you want to tell me about it?"

What I wanted was to turn back the hands of time to before Becca moved to town. And keep them there. It had all been so much simpler then. Back then, no one hated me. And even if they did, I didn't care. "I messed up."

"I see," my father said. He scratched idly at his chin. "The sort of mess-up where you go out with two girls at the same time?"

"No."

"Hmm . . . The kind of mess-up where you try to give a girl a good-night kiss when all they wanted was a good-night wave?"

"No."

"I see." He scratched harder, thinking. "The kind of mess-up where you steal your best friend's girl?"

Geez, there were a lot of ways a guy could mess up. "No. I kinda lied so she would think I was something I wasn't."

"Ah. Like the school jock?"

Dang, why hadn't I gone for that? "I wish. I kinda led her to believe I'm a—a—" the truth was hard to admit, especially to my father "—a vegetarian."

My father coughed. "I'm sorry, did you say vegetarian?"

I nodded.

"I see. You did go for a big one, didn't you? Couldn't you have just told her you were the school jock?"

"She doesn't seem interested in jocks."

"Oh. Then you chose wisely."

Yeah, right. "What do you mean?"

My father smiled. "Well, I just mean as long as you were telling a bald-faced lie, at least you chose one that fit the situation."

I mimicked one of my mother's famous eye rolls.

He let out a laugh. "I didn't say it was the best choice. I just meant at least you were trying to get her attention by focusing on what mattered to her."

I hadn't thought of it like that. "It was stupid."

His smile turned serious. "Yeah, I don't deny that. I take it she found out the truth?"

There seemed no point in covering things up. I spilled the whole story of the days leading up to the parade, and how I somehow believed I'd be able to get away with it without her finding out. I ended with "Clearly, I'm an idiot."

"You must really like this girl to be that brain-addled," my father said, the smile creeping back onto his face. He nudged my knee. "Son, we've all been there."

"I *am* there."

He ran his hand through his hair. "True enough. That's why this is all so confusing, huh?"

That was for darn sure.

"Well, let me tell you a thing or two about women," he continued. "You aren't ever going to understand them. Nor will you ever stop doing stupid, embarrassing things in their presence. It's just a fact of life."

My head hung. This was not the pep talk I needed.

"Stu," my father said, lowering his voice. "You've learned a valuable lesson. Be honest and be yourself. If she doesn't like that, then she's not right for you."

Somehow that did make sense. And sounded a whole lot simpler than the double life I'd been leading. Even if I didn't believe being myself could work with someone like her.

He tapped my shoulder. "Just one more question. What are you going to do now?"

"I don't know. Becca arranged a sit-in at school tomorrow to protest there not being vegetarian entrées at lunch. All my friends are taking part. But I can't pretend to be vegetarian now. She knows the truth."

My father dropped his head in thought. "You realize it pains me to say this. But why don't you take part anyway? I'm sure not all your friends are vegetarian and they're still supporting her cause, right?"

"Yeah, but none of them lied to her."

"What's the worst that can happen?"

"She hates me to my face."

My father stood. "I suppose you're right. That's a risk you'll have to be willing to take." He crossed the room and opened the door, then stopped. "However, maybe there's something we can do to help break the ice."

"What's that?"

"Follow me," he said, a conspiratorial gleam in his eye, "and I'll show you."

45

Friday morning, I spent in class debating whether to follow through on the plan I'd made with my father, or go into hiding. He was either a genius or the idiot father of an even bigger idiot son. The genetic likelihood of us both being idiots sent a shiver through me.

At 11:00, I excused myself to use the restroom. Actually, at 11:00, everyone taking part in the sit-in asked permission to go to the restroom. We had agreed that this was the simplest plan since we were spread out across enough classes to avoid suspicion, although it was not nearly as cool as Ben's idea of bungee jumping out the windows.

I retrieved my backpack from my locker, then headed to the boys' room to put my father's plan into action.

"STU!"

Ben ran up from behind and clapped me on the back. "Are you joining us?"

I held the backpack away from his wandering eyes. "Yeah, I guess so."

"That's so great! Wouldn't be a protest without you."

Ben fell into step beside me. "Maybe they'll bring in fire hoses and spray us. Or police dogs. Or use pepper spray."

Ben had a way of making even the safest things sound dangerous.

"Yeah, I'm sure the police have been waiting for a group of protesting middle schoolers so they can get out their riot gear."

"Do you think?"

"No."

The grin on Ben's face drooped. "Maybe they'll at least have their batons out."

"I don't think so."

He kicked at the floor. "Can't a guy dream?"

I shuddered to think what went on inside his brain while he slept.

We arrived at the boys' room. "Hey, I gotta take care of business." I turned my back before Ben could offer to escort me inside. "See you at the cafeteria."

The swarm of butterflies from Monday returned. They seemed to have brought family. A giant butterfly reunion was taking place inside my stomach. I pulled the rack of ribs costume from my backpack. Only it didn't look like a rack of ribs anymore. I suddenly wondered if anyone would get it. What if they thought I was a walking pile of poop? Against my better judgment, I put on the costume anyway.

The real moment of truth waited. Either I'd be greeted with open arms or turned away with a cold shoulder. I looked in the mirror. One thing was for sure. I wouldn't go unnoticed. Taking a last deep breath, I stepped out into the hallway.

"Dude, that is awesome!"

I should have known Ben would be waiting for me.

"I wondered what was taking you so long." He eyed me up and down again. "Dude, you the man. Or should I say tater tot?"

We hurried toward the cafeteria.

"You're going to be a hit."

"I don't know about that."

Ben eyed me again. "Believe me, you the man."

Everyone else was already inside the cafeteria setting up. When Ben and I entered, all eyes turned. I heard a collective gasp. And then a chorus of whoops and hollers.

"Dude!" Tyler yelled. "You are one hot baked potato!"

Kirsten ran over and patted my melted butter hat. "How did you think of this?" she exclaimed.

"I had a little help."

"It's *AMAZING!*"

Okay, maybe my dad *was* a genius.

Someone handed me a sign that read *Vegetarians Deserve Lunch, Too!!!* The sign looked good next to the *Vegetarians Unite* pin boldly hanging from my potato skin.

A man with a camera approached. "Now that's a picture waiting to be taken."

"He's from the newspaper," Kirsten whispered.

The man gathered everyone around me and then

stepped back to get us all in the picture. "Where's the girl that instigated all this?" he asked.

Kirsten pulled Becca front and center next to me. "Here she is."

"Great," the man said, motioning us to get closer together. "Now everyone lean in around them."

I whispered to Becca, "If you'd rather, I won't take part."

She punched the spongy bulge of my baked potato suit. "And miss seeing you walking around like this?"

She had a point.

The photographer counted down, "Three . . . two . . . one," then snapped a photo. "Perfect. That is perfect."

Kids began streaming into the cafeteria for lunch.

"Places, everyone!" Becca yelled.

The group flew into action, blocking the lunch line with their signs held high.

Becca lifted a megaphone to her lips. "Vegetarians..." she called out.

"Deserve to eat," we answered back.

"Vegetarians . . ." she called again.

"Deserve to eat," we responded.

One of the cooks stepped out of the kitchen. "What is going on here?" she demanded.

"We're protesting the lack of vegetarian entrée options," Becca explained.

The cook looked over at me. "What's that? Your mascot?"

Kirsten stepped next to Becca. "Yep. He's our little baked potato boy."

The cook eyed me again. "Oh, I thought he was a day-old wheat roll."

If you're a cook and you can't tell the difference between a baked potato and a wheat roll, you're probably in the wrong job. Seriously.

I pointed to the green pieces of pipe cleaner sprinkled across the top of my potato skin. "They're chives, ma'am."

That brought a snort from her. "How did I miss that?" She turned her attention back to Becca. "I hate to spoil your fun, but you're blocking the line. If you guys don't move out of the way, I'll have to go get the principal."

Becca gave her a winning smile. "Yes, we're hoping for that."

The cook shook her head and headed toward the office. "Who'd a thunk the day would come when kids started protesting for more vegetables? What is the world coming to?"

A few minutes later, Principal Stevens entered, followed by the cook.

"This is what I was telling you about," said the cook.

"I see," said Principal Stevens.

"Vegetarians . . ." Becca called out on the megaphone.

"DESERVE TO EAT!" we yelled back.

Principal Stevens approached our group. She eyed Becca's megaphone, then my costume. Then took time to read all the signs we were holding. "This is quite an event you've organized," she said at last.

Becca faced her. "We think there should be vegetarian entrée options at lunch," she explained.

The Principal checked out the reader board. It read the same as always: *Hamburger or chicken strips with french fries.* "I see." Her attention returned to our group. "And did you get permission in advance to hold a protest in the lunchroom?"

Becca's face went ashen. "Permission?"

"Especially if anyone left class early to participate."

"It wouldn't be a protest if we got permission," Ben blurted.

"Well, actually that's not true," Principal Stevens said to Ben. "At this school, we expect you to get permission before hosting a protest. Especially one that prevents other students not participating from being able to buy lunch."

I looked around. A line of kids stood, waiting for us to move out of the way.

"But—but," Becca said, "we're trying to change the system."

"I appreciate that," the principal replied. "But you're doing so at the expense of others not part of your cause. They have rights, too."

"But they get lunch every day," Becca responded. "Vegetarians can never buy lunch."

Principal Stevens pondered. "I understand your

point. Let's continue this conversation in my office, shall we?"

"But we're not done protesting," Becca said.

"Hmm . . . tell me, what was the goal of this protest?"

Becca thought for a moment. "Well, we wanted to bring attention to the problem."

"And you've succeeded. If you'll come to my office, perhaps we can do even better than that."

Becca turned to the rest of us. "What do you think?"

Heads nodded. Signs lowered.

"You did it," Kirsten whispered.

Before I could stop myself, I said, "I'm coming with you."

"Thank you," Becca replied.

46

When we got to the main office, Principal Stevens motioned to a couple chairs outside her door. "Please wait here. I need a few minutes."

She entered her office and closed the door behind her.

I tried to squeeze into a chair, but the bulge of my baked potato refused to fit between the arm rests.

"I guess I'll stand," I said, popping back up.

Becca stood next to me while we waited. The zombie warlord in my chest reminded me this was a perfect opportunity to get a few things off my chest. "Uh, uh, I wanted to, uh, to say I was—" I stuttered like a professional stutterer.

Becca put a hand on her hip. "You don't need to apologize for anything, Stu." She avoided my eyes completely. "It doesn't matter."

"No, really," I said. "It does matter. I lied to you about being vegetarian. I'm not. I was really stupid. I'm sorry."

Becca turned toward me. "Why did you tell me you were a vegetarian?"

Why? The blush on my face could have heated a small gymnasium. "Well, I—sometimes you just—the thing is—I think you're—you know—"

Her hand brushed against mine. "You're funny," she said.

"Really?" If there was ever a time I didn't feel funny, it was now.

Becca gave me a nudge. "Yeah, especially when you're embarrassed."

"Then I must be hilarious right now."

She studied the blushing face mounted on a baked potato body. "You have no idea."

I bumped her in return.

"You know," she continued, "it's okay if we're not the same."

I nodded. "I like killing zombies."

"Ooh." Her lips puckered with distaste. "I like playing soccer."

"Really? I like soccer."

She gave me a puzzled look. "Seriously? Or are you just saying that?"

Now why would she wonder that? "No, really. Ben and I have been on the same team since we were little."

"Figures. You two do everything together."

"Pretty much."

We stared out the window at a single cloud floating by. For a moment, time stood still.

A trace of a smile curved Becca's lips. "You know, you might be more vegetarian than you think."

The bacon I had eaten for breakfast jumped to mind. "Maybe. I did eat a piece of kale this week."

"More than that," she said. "You like cheese, don't you?"

"Well, yeah, of course."

"Did you know cheese is vegetarian?"

"Say what?"

She giggled. "Cheese is vegetarian. So are nuts."

"I love nuts. My best friend is one."

She giggled again. "Oreos are vegetarian. So is pudding. Even marshmallows sometimes."

Whoa. My view of vegetarianism was being turned on its head.

"We should have a vegetarian party," she suggested. "With s'mores."

I found myself clapping my hands like Ben. Thank God he wasn't there to witness it.

"That's a great idea! We have a fire pit in our backyard. I'll ask my parents."

The door to Principal Stevens's office opened. "You can come in now," she said.

47

Becca and I stood before Principal Stevens's desk, me looking big, round, and buttery, and her looking, well—like she always does.

Principal Stevens handed us a stack of pink slips. "First things first. I'll let you pass those around."

I looked down at the slips in my hand. Each had a name of someone involved in the sit-in. Each said the same thing: One week's detention. I groaned.

"Principal Stevens," Becca implored. "I'm the one that organized the whole thing. Please don't punish everyone."

"I'm okay being punished," I added. There were worse things than spending a week after school in detention with Becca.

Principal Stevens gave us her don't-push-me smile. "I appreciate the thought, but the reality is that every one of you cut class. And everyone will have to pay the price. However," she continued, "during this afternoon's detention, I've invited Ms. Halliday, the head cook, to meet with you. I just got off the phone with her. She's open to working with you on a solution to provide more vegetarian entrée options."

Becca's jaw dropped. "Really? That's awesome!"

"For next time, arrange with me before holding any more protests. Okay?"

We both nodded.

Becca looked ready to burst on our way back to class.

"Can you believe that?" she kept repeating.

"Yeah, you did it."

She beamed at me. "We all did it. Together."

My backpack was waiting for me at my locker. "I'm going to change before going back to class."

"Thanks for coming with me," Becca said.

"Yeah," I replied, sticking my hand out.

She took my hand and giggled. "Thank you, sir."

The absurdity of shaking hands set my cheeks burning again. "Thank you," I squeaked. My father's words returned to mind. He hadn't been joking. I really was destined to do stupid things around girls for the rest of my life. I took my backpack and headed for the boys' room to change. At the doorway, I turned. Becca was still standing next to my locker. As if on cue, we both waved goodbye.

My walk home that afternoon was an absolute pleasure. Along the way, I counted four baby ducks and helped a little girl back on her bike. I also waved to an elderly man while humming "Happy Birthday" for absolutely no reason. Some things just can't be helped.

After I got home, I finished my homework in record time. Ben came over after dinner and we finished level twenty-eight of *Death Intruders 4*. And I introduced him to my new favorite vegetarian dessert: s'mores.

"This vegetarian stuff is for real," he said between gooey mouthfuls.

For a kid with an oversized head and a thirst for

chasing zombies with chain saws, he could be down-right poetic.

"My mom found vegetarian marshmallows," I said, licking marshmallow cream off my lips. "So it really is for real."

48

Monday lunch came like any other lunch except for a few small changes. Ben, Tyler, Ryan, and I sat together like always. Except that we were now sharing a table with Kirsten, Becca, Gretchen, Annie, and about four hundred other people who had become our closest friends. And the crazy thing was that I didn't mind any of them. Even Jackson. He waved from the far end, surrounded by roughly half the girls in the school. Best of all, my baked potato costume was a thing of the past.

"Hey, look," Ben said, holding up the front page of the Sunday paper. "It's what's for dinner."

Almost a thing of the past. The photo on the front page featured me in my baked potato costume sur-rounded by the rest of the protestors. The caption read

Vegetarian protest leads to school lunch menu changes.

I took a bite of the grilled cheese sandwich on my tray. The sign over the lunch line read *Today's specials: hamburger or grilled cheese.* "Yep, it's all about the vegetarian."

Ben swiped my milk and took a swig. An empty carton landed back on my tray. "Yep, all about the vegetarian," he agreed.

One of these days, I'm gonna stuff that kid into a milk carton. If only I can get his head to fit.

Kirsten gave Becca a high five. "We're real change makers."

"Amen," Ben added. "Anyone got change? I want to get a juice from the vending machine."

Becca leaned over and held out a bag of peas.

"Want a Joe's Smokin' Pea?" she asked.

"No, thank you," I replied.

She gave me her best hurt-puppy-dog look. "Really? Not even one?"

Puppies are the worst. I took a pea and popped it in my mouth. Mother of all peas. How could anyone eat those things? I gulped it down, followed by Ben's juice. "Those are the worst things ever. I'd rather suck on Ben's socks."

"And I'm not even wearing socks," Ben added.

That brought a groan from the crowd.

Becca and I exchanged smiles. It felt good to be myself. Almost as good as it would feel to finish level thirty of *Death Intruders 4*. Ben and I were planning to do that after school. Right after detention, of course.

The bell rang. A collective sigh rose from the table as we packed up to go.

"Don't forget you're all invited to my house Friday night for a bonfire and s'mores," I called out to the group. "And not just any s'mores: vegetarian s'mores."

"Wouldn't miss it," Ben called back.

Becca joined the rest in giving me a thumbs-up.

On our way to class, I pondered if I had to choose one moment to relive over and over for eternity, which moment would I choose? The day Ben and I met? Eh. My last birthday party? Probably not. Riding on my father's parade float? No. I looked over at Becca, giggling at some joke Ben had just made. I don't know. Maybe I'd choose this moment.

Becca bumped my arm. "See you later."

"See you."

Yeah, I guess today's lunch would be all right. I clapped Ben on the shoulder. Or maybe tomorrow's. Or maybe even Friday's bonfire. What could be better than an eternity filled with s'mores? Ben gave me a peace sign and disappeared into his next class.

Who knew what the future held? I pulled my hood back. Guess I'd find out soon enough.

Acknowledgments

Writing a story AND making it funny is like adding an extra twist to a high dive. The effort is bound to bring gasps from the crowd, either in awe or alarm. Thankfully, my plunge from platform to pool occurred with the help of an amazing supporting cast. I'd like to take a moment and thank them.

First, thanks to the town of Sequim for giving me the small-town space I needed to stumble my way out of boyhood, even if the journey is still a work in progress. BTW, the Irrigation Festival and parade are for real: irrigationfestival.com. Make your reservations early.

Where would I be without my amazing agent, Ammi-Joan Paquette? Probably flipping burgers at this very moment. Mmm . . . burgers . . . Anyway, Joan was foolhardy enough to stand by me when no one else found my writing the least bit interesting. She alone kept the faith and kept reminding me to stop sniveling and keep writing. Thank you, Joan!

I live between two careers these days and Erin

Cunningham is the person who single-handedly keeps all the details straight so that neither world collapses from its own weight. Thank you, Erin, for wearing oh-so-many hats and making each of them look like a perfect accessory.

Thank you to the Tighty Writeys, an inspiring collection of children's authors who meet regularly to tell each other how awful our works in progress really are—all done with love, friendship, and mutual admiration. Thank you, Dana, Curtis, Laurie, Kevan, Allyson, Lois, Jeanie, and Dori for believing in me even before Joan did. And that's saying something.

Thank you, Cathy, Susan, and Louise for your constant encouragement and feedback. And Conrad, every word that comes out of your mouth is a dissertation on writing. I've learned so much, and don't in any way blame you for how *Stu* turned out.

I would know nothing about writing for children if not for the dedicated, and mostly volunteer, folks at SCBWI. What an amazing organization of children's authors and illustrators.

I'm blessed to have a family who are not the least bit

annoyed at the time I spend locked away in my office laughing at my own jokes. Thank you, Kelly, Anna, and Paul for being the most beautiful, loving, and understanding family a boy—I mean "man"—could ever want. Burgers are on the BBQ, and veggies too, of course. . . .

I wrote the first draft of *Stu Truly* while coaching my son's seventh-grade basketball team, the Trailblazers. Paul and his friends reminded me weekly what it was like being tossed into the early throes of manhood. No, none of the characters are based on you guys. Yes, all of the characters are based on you guys.

The person most responsible for me being an author is my middle school English teacher, Mrs. Verstegen. Anything you like about this novel is due to her. Anything you don't like about this novel is also due to her. Sorry, Mrs. Verstegen, but someone has to be held accountable. I'm so glad it could be you!

Sometimes a book needs an extra boot in the backside to get its act together. Tamra Tuller was the perfect boot for *Stu*. Thanks, Tamra, for your expert guidance and for treating me like a professional long before I felt like one.

Stu got his lucky break from my oh-so-fabulous editor, Sonali Fry. Thanks, Sonali, for believing in a story about a boy, his first crush, and a meat float. Yikes, when I put it like that . . . Special thanks to Dave Barrett for your copyediting and proofing expertise. And thanks to the marketing and publicity team, Gayley Avery, Nadia Almahdi, and Crystal McCoy for your over-and-above efforts, and for calling me adorable after our first meeting.

The Cool Whip on top of the sundae came from Simini Blocker's artwork and senior designer Rob Wall's cover design. Thank you both for making the book a visual treat!

There is nothing scarier when writing a children's book than having actual children read it. Thank you, teachers Nathan and Shannon, for reading an early draft to your classes, and for your insightful feedback. And remember, what happened in the first draft stays in the first draft. . . .

And thank you, dear readers, for joining me on Stu's cringe-worthy journey from childhood to early manhood. I hope his story brought a little humor and perspective to your own journey. In the words of the celebrated poet: "Puberty is best endured with sharp wit and selective memory loss." Okay, no poet ever said that. But it's still true.